TRYSTS

TRYSTS

A Triskaidecollection
of Queer and Weird Stories

BY STEVE BERMAN

 2001

ISBN: 1-59021-000-X

Lethe Press
102 Heritage Avenue
Maple Shade, NJ 08052
www.lethepress.com

Design and composition by Sandy Freeman
Cover image by Matt Bauer
Cover design by Sara Cucinotta
Manufactured in the United States of America

For my father who taught me
how to dream and scheme,
for my mother who showed me
that love is not a myth,
to both of you I dedicate this book.

"Alec," said Richard. "It really isn't safe for you to be going out alone here after dark. People get wild, and not everyone knows who you are yet."

"No one knows who I am."

ELLEN KUSHNER,
Swordspoint

"Wait! You haven't seen anything." She put down her books by the graveyard gate and swinging it open went inside. "You have to look at the tombstones. They're all weird."

JOHN COYNE,
Hobgoblin

ACKNOWLEDGEMENTS

AS THIS ANTHOLOGY CONTAINS WORK WRITTEN over the past few years, it may be impossible to thank everyone who has offered encouragement and help.

First and foremost, all blame for any success Tryst might have falls on Holly Black. Without her I'd be lost and many of these stories would never have been finished. She knew when to harass and when to praise. I could not ask for a better friend or confidant.

Mike Thomas, who has been a devoted e-mail friend over the years and has seen too much of my work to ever remain sane, never was afraid to tell me when my grammar was horrible. Jed Hartman, one of the kind editors at Strange Horizons, a premier web-based magazine of speculative fiction, helped to guide several of these stories from raw draft to finished work.

I cannot forget my cadre of friends that listened whenever I rambled about some new story intended for Trysts: Evan and Natalie Cutler, Judy Paterson, Theo Black, Bill Hadsell, and Frank Slattery for his business advice.

To those lost or left behind, I miss their role in my life: Dave Pinto and Michael Carte, who have always served as inspiration, especially at my most lonesome moments.

Sandy Freeman and Sara Cucinotta are responsible for the incredible design of the book, inside and out. I would also like to thank Matt Bauer. He's the talented artist who created the piece on the cover. Not only is he creative, but he's one of the sweetest guys around.

FOREWORD

IT'S ONLY A MATTER OF TIME BEFORE THE WORD tryst is listed in the dictionary as obsolete, antiquated, or—my favorite—archaic. Which is sad, really, because there is no better single syllable to describe a stolen moment of passion.

Daydreamers like the word. As a teen, I did an awful lot of daydreaming; being gay and closeted meant that the only trysts I could have were in my imagination. But simple games of pretend quickly became unsatisfying—idle thoughts of the boy who sat next to me in class leaning over to kiss me were not enough. Soon I began to invent romantic rendezvous: we would find ourselves alone together, then we would talk—bits of conversation that made me shiver—and finally, well, the climax of our little meeting. Day and night I replayed these dreams, changing scenes, endlessly trying to perfect them. Without realizing it, I had become a writer, creating and revising characters, setting, dialogue, and plots.

Of course if you don't have to worry about reality, then there are no limits to what kind of tryst can be had. I have always been thrilled by thoughts of magic and monsters; one of my fondest memories as a child was sitting down next to my mother and watching the old black-and-white horror movies on television. So my trysts quickly became more fanciful, even adventurous, than just two boys in love. Often there were secret passageways or ghosts or fiends.

The Encyclopedia of Fantasy defines Dark Fantasy as a genre in which stories incorporate a sense of horror or unease but are clearly fantastical. That is a good description of my work. Like characters in

Gothic fiction, my characters are often confronted with dismal situations and surroundings that mirror the turmoil they suffer inside. Some are tormented by being different; all feel the pain of loneliness.

There are thirteen stories here, all told—which makes this, to adapt another archaic word, a triskaidecollection. Not every culture thinks thirteen is an unlucky number. I share that view; thirteen seems more thrilling than awful. Each tale revolves around a tryst. It may be a chance meeting which incites new passion, or a pair re-igniting lost love. But remember that these stories are weird as well as queer; as you read them, you may find that sometimes two people can come together in strange (and even unnatural) ways.

Steve Berman
sberman8@yahoo.com
July 2001

CONTENTS

BEACH 2

DANIEL HAD LEFT THE BEACH HOUSE A LITTLE after midnight, but now it was almost two o'clock. His senses were oddly awakened. The shades of dark gray and black were all new, perhaps had never even been named before. Sand was washed over with spray until it was all overcome by the night sky. The only real colors came from over his shoulder, the garish flashing bulbs and neon of the casinos.

There were odd sounds and smells, too. The surf had so many different roars; like snowflakes, no two were exactly alike. The rushing water brought from the ocean the stink of seaweed as well as the cleansing odor of salt. The casinos' distant din reached out over the beach, perfectly matched by an atmosphere of dinners, cheap buffet meatloaf vying against trout amandine. Even the sand had a smell, and the boardwalk itself. Clean and seasoned from so many summer years, and layers of suntan oil pounded into the grit and wood by countless feet.

All in all, it felt wonderful to be out there. At least until he looked at his watch and saw he had only twenty minutes left. He turned in the direction of the beach house. It was out of sight, quiet and slumbering. He wasn't sure if he could go back inside.

THAT AFTERNOON, THE TWO COUPLES HAD JUST been settling in. Well, maybe not couples—Susan had brought along this guy, Seth, that Daniel and Hilary hadn't met before, but it seemed obvious to Daniel that Seth was nothing more than a friend of Susan's. Maybe just a passing fad of a friend. But it was her folks' beach house, so she could invite anyone she wanted along for the weekend.

Hilary instantly disliked Seth. When she and Daniel were together in the guest bedroom unpacking, she had begun her usual routine. Daniel had become so used to the routine that he only started listening on the third comment.

"And what's with the piercings? Is Susan into skaters now?"

Daniel emptied her suitcase while she sat on the queen-sized bed. "I don't think they're dating." He carefully put each folded silken undergarment in the top drawer of the dresser. Then he started on the bathing suits and tops, and finally the skirts that needed to be hung in the walk-in closet.

"I hope not. He gives me the creeps. I think he was staring at me."

Daniel chuckled. Not that the idea was silly, because he knew Hilary was attractive. Many guys told him that. They especially loved her legs, which had always seemed a bit too long for him. But no, he didn't think Seth was staring at her. Seth had hazel eyes. And maybe used a touch of brown eyeliner. "Don't let him bother you. The weather is supposed to be great, you wanted a tan to show off to your co-workers, and everything will be fine." He hugged her—not too tightly, as he still held a coat hanger in one hand draped with her cotton dress, the one with the embroidered neckline.

When he went downstairs, Seth handed him a full wine glass. Daniel smiled back and told himself again that everything *would* be fine.

DANIEL STARTED TO WALK BACK ALONG THE shoreline, where the sand lay heavy and dark. His sandals were open to every grain, and when the rushing water came rhythmically in, he shivered at the coolness.

Not that far, just over a few ridges and a jetty. So what if he ran across anyone out here? He was only out because he couldn't sleep. He rarely slept well these days.

AFTER A DAY SPENT SOAKING IN THE SUN, THE four returned to the beach house, parched. Hilary had turned a shade redder than she wanted; she blamed the manufacturer of the department-store-brand oil she had lathered herself with. She had developed a mantra: "SPF 15, my ass."

While Hilary took a cooling soak in the tub, Daniel helped Susan and Seth with dinner. He had never grilled before—it had always been his father's cooking territory, never relinquished—and so he worried that he'd lose one of the skewered shrimp down into the hot coals. Thankfully, Seth stood by his shoulder, helping, showing him how to carefully turn the food and to keep it from being burned. Susan drifted by and winked at both of them, as if she knew a secret, perhaps one about the giant salad bowl she carried.

Out on the deck, they all sat down to eat. Hilary's job turned out to be pouring wine. She was very good at it and became almost chatty as she refilled glasses.

When the dishes were cleared, the night sky had turned bruise-purple and the stars were just beginning to shine. Seth had left the table and leaned against the deck's railing, one bare arm dangling over the side. Daniel wondered if by summer's end Seth's skin would reach the same caramel color as his hair.

A cool breeze off the ocean wrapped around all of them. Hilary shivered, a silent cue to all of them that she wanted to go inside.

Back in the den, they stole the cushions from the sofas and lounged on the carpeted floor, discussing what to do next.

Daniel picked up a nearby chamois pillow. "We could build a fort." There were some laughs.

Hilary had her hand on his bare knee; she gave it a squeeze. "Is there any place to go dancing? Danny and I took lessons for a wedding last month." She smiled at him. A nice smile, one of the infectious ones she rationed out. "He's really good."

Susan shook her head. "Nothing, really, in A.C." Her tone was curiously flat.

"I brought something."

All heads turned to Seth, who looked to Daniel suddenly impish, especially with his soft brown bangs and the golden rings along his ears.

"Hold on." He rose and left the room.

"Well, what do you think of him?" Susan asked conspiratorially, leaning in close.

Why did Daniel think the question was aimed at him? He opened his mouth, but Hilary answered for him. "Okay, but a little young for you, isn't he?"

"What's wrong with twenty-four? Your guy isn't much older."

Seth returned with a board-game box that had seen better days. The edges were bandaged with masking tape. "Here we are. Something different."

Susan fairly squealed when Seth lifted off the top and revealed a Ouija board. Daniel heard Hilary's soft "ugh."

"I've had it since I was a kid." Seth had a wide grin. Daniel saw that his bottom teeth were crooked.

"Oh, let's play." Susan helped to take the board out.

"Shouldn't we dim the lights?" Daniel regretted speaking, for Hilary gave him a look.

A harmless game. At least, that's what the small print on the underside of the lid promised. Susan insisted that two people had to work the small plastic guide, the planchette, but Daniel did not recall reading that in the instructions.

Susan and Seth went first. They knelt close over the board and laid their fingers lightly on the planchette. When it started to move, Hilary whispered to Daniel, "I think the only spirit pushing that thing is the bottle of vino next to Sue." Her lips tickled the sensitive skin of his ear.

Seth spoke aloud every letter, number, and symbol, in a mock-eerie tone. Susan's laughter, heavy and alcohol-rich, often skidded the planchette out of control. Daniel grinned madly. The very last movement landed on the question mark—a fitting end, as they then spent over twenty minutes trying to unravel the jumble's meaning over soft cheese, apple slices, and lots of cheap, dry wine.

"Your turn," Susan said to Daniel and Hilary.

"No, I don't like this crap."

Daniel began to beg her, but she just shook her head, causing long brown strands of hair to get in her face. He saw it was pointless.

"I'll do it with you."

Daniel blinked suddenly. Then he saw Seth slide the planchette over to him. He blushed.

For both men to move the piece from opposite sides would have been awkward, so Seth stood up and moved around next to where Daniel sat.

Daniel caught a whiff of Seth's cologne. It hung lightly about the man's shoulders and neck and smelled wonderful. He took several deep breaths of it.

"Ready?"

Daniel nodded and gently put his fingers on the plastic piece, finding it too small for Seth not to touch him.

Daniel struggled to keep his eyes on the board. But he could barely pay any attention to the black script or numerals, even as he felt the planchette move. He closed his eyes—the safest path, he decided—and let Seth guide him.

B. E. A. C. H. Then the planchette reached the 2 and stopped.

"*Beach 2?* What the hell does that mean?" Hilary drew back, finally removing her hand from Daniel's leg. She nearly knocked over a half-empty bottle of California white.

Daniel was silent. He rubbed the tips of his fingers idly, secretly remembering Seth's presence.

They spent far less time interpreting this second prophecy. Susan had reached the point where any more drink made her more tired than giddy. Seth had become silent, fingering the silver ring around his thumb, taking it off and putting it on, and rolling it in his palm.

Daniel faked a yawn. His mind turned over one thought—Beach 2—again and again, like the movement of that ring.

"Tired, sweetie?" Hilary squeezed his arm. Her breath didn't smell from the wine, which he thought strange considering how much she had drunk.

He nodded. "We're going to turn in," he told Susan and Seth.

"So early?" But Susan said it haphazardly, almost breathless.

As they undressed in the guest room, both had eyes more on the bed than on each other. The sheets, so glaringly white, seemed more inviting to each of them than the common sight of the other naked. When they finished undressing, Daniel made the attempt to be amorous, cupping his favorite of her breasts, the one with the dark freckle. She sighed, then shuddered. But when he touched her back, she winced at sunburn.

"Sorry," he said, and turned out the light. He heard her ease onto the mattress, then the whisper of the cotton sheets as they slipped over her bare skin.

"What's wrong?"

He realized he still stood naked by the bed. He shook his head, then realized the gesture would be missed in the darkness. "Nothing."

The creak of springs. "Nothing's keeping you from coming to bed?" Her voice was more tired than grumpy.

He struggled for an answer, one that would at least sound right. Before he could stop himself, he said the name that had been on his lips all day, all night.

"What did he say to you?" Her tone chilled. "It was about me, right?"

"No." It came out more like a sigh.

"Then what was it?"

It was the promise of softness by the fine hairs along Seth's forearms, the thought of running his hands up the length of those arms until he came to the wide shoulders. The chance to bury his head in the crook of Seth's neck and finally taste the warmth the sun had left his skin.

He paced about the room without realizing it. "I'm not used to guys like him." An honest answer, something he could say without regret.

If she understood what he was saying, she gave no clue. "Maybe we should just go back home tomorrow."

He sat down on the bed. He could dimly make out where she lay and reached out with his hand, touching her arm. "No. I want to stay."

She stayed silent for a minute. He felt her fingers lightly brush against his forehead. "You're sweating." She then rolled over, her back to him.

The bedsheets felt as cool as they looked.

NEARLY BACK TO THE BEACH HOUSE, DANIEL stopped one last time. He trembled, but not because of the cool breeze. All he had to do to keep life sane was go back, slip into bed, put his arm around her, and forget. Did he really want to abandon everything he knew, to leave a life he had grown, if not fond of, at least accustomed to? He should force himself to follow his tracks back. He found them, off to his right, his footprints deep in the sand. At least, they looked like his. They would lead back to Hilary and perhaps that day when they'd dance at their own wedding.

But he ached when he thought about the future. He had so many urges, none of them easy to define, not even his turbulent thoughts of Seth. It seemed crazy to let any of them take hold, but these days he constantly imagined things. None of them led to a self he could clearly picture.

HE NEVER FELL ASLEEP. INSTEAD, DANIEL stared at the walls, at the ceiling, trying not to envision any more of Seth than a vague wanting. His hands wandered underneath the pillow, along the mattress edge, and too often down his own chest, down past his waist. He would find them there by surprise and then stare at the digital clock on the night table. Next to him came the gentle wheeze and movement that told him Hilary was deep asleep. At twelve, he slowly lifted himself up and looked down at her.

Her mouth hung partly open. She liked to be kissed like that, he remembered. Hilary liked to be woken with a kiss, as if her life were a fairy tale and each morning the start of a new day. He envied that fantasy. Envied that it was mostly fulfilled.

Fifteen minutes later he slipped out from under the covers and pulled on the shirt and shorts he had worn that day. They still carried the warmth from his body. He carried his sandals and crept to the door. As if part of the conspiracy, the hinges didn't creak.

The kitchen had a screen door that led to the beach. He was across the room before he realized that the silhouette at the table was alive. He stopped dead, holding his breath.

"It's a nice night for a walk." Susan's voice was so deep that it took him several moments to realize it was her.

"Why are you doing this?" Daniel asked. How long had she been planning all this?

"I'm right, aren't I?" She moved closer, into his path. Though it was too dark to see, he could imagine her eyes, watery with all the wine, perhaps decorated with Seth's handiwork.

WHERE THE TALL GRASS CLAIMED THE TOP OF the beach, Daniel saw a small orange glow floating. The breeze brought the scent of sweet smoke to him. How like Seth to smoke cloves. What taste did that leave in the mouth?

Daniel did not bother looking at his watch. Whether or not it was 2 a.m., he knew deep down it was time to walk up there, to the edge of the beach, to where the sand promised to be warm.

STORMED AND
TAKEN IN PRAGUE

WOULD IT HELP TO TELL HOW HAUNTED THIS city is? Walk the quiet, lonely streets and listen. Soft sighs and sobs and whispers hidden in the sound of a footfall, the drip of rain, the rustle of cloth. Each building wears a patina created from smoke and acid rain and simply too many years left standing.

Most nights I wander, taking the wrong alleyways back from wherever, all to avoid my lonesome rented flat. I have been in Prague for three months but I doubt I'll ever leave. So many small streets call out, seem to breathe. I can find old bulletholes in walls, marks that threaten to add new carvings to the marble like the crudest of chisels. Why is everything so haunted here?

Back in the States, I heard so many things about this city. Beer so cheap that pocket change would last the whole night. Bottles of absinthe waiting to be downed. Clubs that pounded with trembling music and fevered bodies. Crowds of the eager young looking to make their lives mean something, if only for a night. So I left the uncomfortable boredom that had held me for so long and traveled across the Atlantic looking to claim something lurid for myself.

I had the funds to avoid the cramped rooms filled with bedrolls and blankets that other ex-patriots faced. I rented a small penthouse suite fallen on bad times. The building might once have been grand. Or else victim to an artist with no taste. Hard to tell with all the layers of soot and dismay covering the ornamentation along its sides. What most captivated my eye amid that grotesque current state was along the door. A figure reposing against the frame. Streaks of marble for hair. Or merely cracks in the stone. The turn of a thigh eaten away by pollution. I would return home, my mouth and head thick with the taste of vodka, and spend nearly an hour staring at the work. But I never could reach past the grime.

I DOUBT THAT THE CZECH SCRAWL OVER THE club's old doors actually translated to Stormed and Taken; for all I knew it could have meant Sweatshop Demands Blood. You don't need to understand any of the locals to survive here. Just have an empathy for situations that might occur. So I think it was my fellow ex-patriots that had dubbed the club. By the decibel level leaking through the old brickwork, I commended their choice.

The club's owner was a loathsome, middle-aged Frenchman who barely fit in his outfit of dark silk and metal clasps. Everyone had on their lips his years of suffering through the rigors of art school, until his escape to Eastern Europe where his spirit could finally go unfettered by demands. Perhaps. Seems to me that a little learning in a Third World country could be stretched to be recognized as genius.

I barely glanced at the catwalks and the iron circular stairways. Hastily constructed frescos along the walls were fine. But trees fashioned from clay and bits of sticks, all set to rise from the scuffed floor and entangle the platforms?

But one did not go to the S&T to appreciate the trappings. What had kept it alive after four months was a raw and basic draw far better than loud music and cheap drink. Back in the States, it would have been raided, the owners and patrons lynched perhaps.

The Frenchman's one bit of creativity was to adorn the club with rented bodies. The most alluring locals, each a living bas-relief standing naked except for layers of plaster and porcelain masks. One to a niche, each still until you glance away and turn back to find yourself staring at their new pose and accompanying innuendo.

During an evening, a statue would sneak off its stand and waylay a dancer, bringing them back to their hole for the fuck of the evening. Though supposedly random, everyone knew that gratuity to the Frenchman could ensure that a hungry soul never exited the S&T. With flesh always in demand, the club never risked becoming passé.

My first night I dedicated to pure ego, wanting to be freely chosen as one of the lucky few to appreciate the local art up close.

If my sense of reality was any more skewed by what I drank that evening, I would have to say that Prague was kept inside those doors that night. The floor could be glimpsed only as a pause between footwork. The floor pounded with dancing feet, the walls echoed the music.

Still, I barely glanced at anything other than the prizes in their niches. So much flesh and muscle and curves. All barely hidden under the finest of white coatings. I ached to touch and taste one.

Around me youths dressed like dead poets and leather ghosts danced. The timid ones hung in clumps, looking about, never daring to embrace serious sin. My eyes grew more wet and wide with every shot of vodka and sight I took in.

The crowd around me began to part; a golem strode the dance floor. One of the statues on the prowl, a tall woman, who still held a paper-mache tree branch in her left hand. She idly swung the stick before her like a dowsing rod. My heart skipped out of whatever doleful beat the DJ played when I saw her heading straight for me. I did not mind handling a woman tonight.

But before she could take me, a weasel rushed in to coil around her. One of the Frenchman's latest cronies, some little man from South America with an excessive appetite. I let myself imagine that the statue gave me a brief look of misery and lost joy while leading the weasel back to her niche. Some small comfort to know his trendy just-bought clothes would be ruined from the handling.

I kept to myself, bitter the rest of the night.

After drinking too much I barely managed the walk back to my flat. Every step was a mixture of sway and lean and near-fall, as my hands touched the buildings along the streets, my feet stomping through dark puddles on the road. Finally I found myself home, a revelation that I had ever found my way back. I rested against the wall, my face against the cool stonework. One hand near my cheek, the fingers idly scratching at the loose mortar. Something began to give. Dust and bits of stone fell, and I looked up, shocked at what I had done.

I had torn loose some of the age from the doorway, revealing more of the old design. Something creamy and smooth. Perhaps a shoulder. My fingers dug around it, hoping to uncover more, but my nails only cracked and bled as the rest was too solid to move. Whatever form was in the cocoon would stay another night.

In Prague, the days are for exploring and a bit of drink with lunch. Those who spent the night in excess wander about like hollow shells, wincing every so often at some unseen slight. Their bloodshot eyes dart about with concern. Battle fatigue, I suppose. I had physically recovered well enough, but my foul mood was still evident by the death of any taste all afternoon. Every bite and swallow became a chore of boredom. Tonight had to be when I sampled one of the statues from the S&T. The thought of waiting another week seemed too much to bear.

I was too eager to begin the night, showing up an hour before the crowd so that I might admire more of the decor. I avoided gawking like a circus mark, instead letting my eye fall on each bit of still flesh with an artisan's approval.

This time I made sure that no little vermin would get in the way. I made the effort to buy the obnoxious cronies of the Frenchman drinks. Only a few drops of the cheapest rat poison to each and every cup, an old trick I learned from my days as a bar-back in New Orleans. Not that they'd be dead, but it's enough to ensure stomach cramps and leave them dry heaving until the early morning hours. I made sure to walk away from the bar before the ill effects started.

A smell first alerted me. Almost musty but not unpleasant. I saw the faces of the crowd around me shift to masks of envy as they looked behind me. When I turned I could only stare.

My eyes were held by the lines of muscle along a firm chest, down arms and legs wrapped in black ribbon and dusted with plaster. The young man had all his body hair shaved except for a long black mane, slicked back. He lifted a hand for me to take. I did not hesitate.

The grip was rough and tight leaving me hard in an instant, basking in the reaction of those around me as I was led off the dance floor and into an alcove no deeper than a yard.

The youth held me tight, my face pressed hard against his strong chest. Hearing his heartbeat disappointed me for it betrayed the illusion of being fucked by something inhuman.

The smell of plaster mingled with the scents of sex, of semen and secretions, of sweat and sighs. I breathed it all in as rough hands tore my clothes off me.

My first taste of him was rich. The Frenchman must have made sure that the plaster was flavored so as not to deter the lips and tongue. My hands and face traveled up and down the length of his body, never removing more than a fine layer of the plaster.

And then he took what he wanted, pushing me against the wall, cold against my naked front, my ass kneaded by his hands. I felt no breath against my neck even though he was close, so close that my skin itched from where he touched me.

A moment later I felt something heated and harsh impale me. I would have cried out but a hand was locked over my mouth, cutting off any gasp. A deep pain, running all through me, sending ripples through my body. If I wasn't crushed against the stonework on every thrust as he fucked me hard, I would have collapsed. But thankfully I could not move. Trapped, I let myself indulge in the raw intensity of living and surviving when all around me suffered.

I do not know how long he lasted. I had already sprayed cum all over the wall and myself. When finally released, I would have fallen had he suddenly not caught me, in the most gentle of hold, licking my cheek of the sweat.

Wet trails went down my back and thighs. I looked down to see that some were bright red. My rear side must be marked with lines from sweet abrasion.

I weakly attempted to dress myself, often looking back up towards the object of my desire, who had become still once more. All the blood I had donated to provide lube was staining my shirt and jeans. I was a virgin to the Storm no longer.

The walk back to my flat was spent in long remembrance of the act. I had finally discovered something overwhelming enough to capture my thoughts totally. I gave only a moment's regard to the stone of home. The blocks seemed in bad shape, the steps gave a little under my feet, and crumbs of mortar fell upon me as I opened the front door.

THE DAYS SEEMED FAR TOO LONG UNTIL THE weekend, an imagined mental torment. I found myself walking past the slumbering S&T, seeing how its outside facade looked under daylight, wondering if the statues ever went home... and could I walk them there. During this time I also made a mental note to seek another place to live. The building looked more disheveled than ever, like an old person throwing off a set of worn clothes. The only good that came from the decay was the unearthing of the sculpture framing the door. A figure with arms wrapped around itself, though not enough had crumbled away to reveal sex or design. But the whole lent a sad air of lost art to the place, a moving greeting to me whenever I entered.

I became a regular of the club, if not an all too willing sacrifice to any statue that would take me. They all came in so many stances, so many builds, that to say I enjoyed them all was foolish. My emotions, my hormones reacted upon stimulus with frightening speed.

Afterwards I would feel scared at how easily I lent myself to any of them. But the scene was too addicting, so I ignored the nightmares. I disregarded the scars on my body that were a mark of my patronage, my being taken.

My last night at the S&T, I could barely rise from the floor after being pushed from an alcove. The Frenchman had the hired help gently escort me to a back room so that with iodine and bandages I could patch myself together to accept the gracious paid drinks he gave to a favored customer. I headed home wondering if I'd collapse along the way.

The cool breeze that night rushed my scratched skin and made me feel delirious from the raw intensity. I think I began to cry, but at what I could not tell. On the steps to my building, I raised a hand to wipe my eyes clear, when a familiar touch took hold of my wrist: the rough texture, firm grip, no warmth. Had one of the statues from the S&T followed me home? Perhaps even the one I had been with that night.

I stopped the tears and grinned at the thought of finally sharing my dim penthouse. But turning, I found the pale gray hand that held me led along a granite arm to the wall, where it met the caryatid. The face, still sexless under a cover of ash and grime turned to me, causing debris to fall at my feet. Then I was released, though I did not pull away; the shock of the sight still held my feet in place as I watched the figure's free hand rise to its head and begin to scrape away and free its features. I stumbled back, moving away from my home.

I spent almost a day curled in an alley near the club. I sought to convince myself that a monster did not lurk outside my apartment. Would the craftsman of old Prague truly adorn their homes with something horrid? What would I see when the stone sheets that wrapped my golem crumbled away? Perhaps something so startling in its beauty that I'd lose all my will and utterly succumb.

And now the end. The haunt is free. I am so weary of standing in the shadows and betraying my inner wants and desires. The doorway to my building has collapsed; the rubble before the entrance has been cleared away for me to come inside. Though my window is dark, I know something waits up there for me. And yet, I feel only a twinge of fear. Has my sin only been skirting the edge of the storm, never really braving the turbulent winds surrounding the eye? All sorts of thoughts make me stifle a mad laugh. An image intrudes upon my mind: would the lumpy mattress support us if I was taken to bed? And if that mass of stuffing and springs could not survive the embrace, how would I?

HIS PAPER DOLL

"RICHIE, WHAT ARE YOU DOING?" HAN FLOPPED down on the bed next to me, nearly causing me to ruin the delicate cutting job I was intent on.

"Making voodoo dolls." I hadn't turned around when he'd come into my room.

"Yeah, right." I should have expected the blasé reaction. He picked up the magazine I had been using as source material. "This the latest *XY*?"

I nodded, trying to trim with scissors around the curve of a forearm I liked. It had a neat tribal tattoo around the bicep. The boy it had belonged to looked up from the page, blissfully unaware of what I had done to him.

"You're trashing it!" Han held up one glossy page I had already performed surgery on. He peered at me through the cut-out.

"Han..." His full name is Han-Kyoung. His father's American and his mother's from Korea. That makes a gorgeous mutt. I'm taller than he is, but he has all this spiky cool hair, so I guess that makes us even.

He turned a few pages, coming to another photo spread of gorgeous guys being playful on the beach, laughing and grinning on the

17

sand while they practically groped each other. I hadn't cut that one yet. "I want to look like those boys."

"You already do." He truly did. He was a boi with an i that stood for "i can't believe he's so yummy." 'Cept that he was my best friend so he was only sorta yummy. More like small-print yummy.

Me, well, I'd probably never be pictured in any mag. I'm the sort where you focus only on a feature. Nice green eyes. Good smile. Never the total package. Han's a total package.

"Yeah, but they all have their arms around other beautiful boys. I have no one."

Inwardly, I groaned. This again. What had it been, three weeks since he hooked up? "So make a doll with me."

He rolled over on his back. "Nah. You're so weird." He began paging through the magazine.

I'm constantly being asked about Han and me. People don't ever get that we're just friends. The closest we've ever come to doing anything was hanging all over each other, sweaty and rolling in a pile, at this one rave.

They don't see that Han needs someone who won't screw him over, who will be true, if that word even means anything anymore. He needs a friend, one who won't care if he does something stupid or wrong.

I tore off a strip of clear tape and added the arm to the pretty little Frankenstein in my hands. I needed Han as a guide through queer teen life, someone who I could share all my thoughts and feelings with.

"So why the doll?"

"I told you, it's a voodoo doll. I read this book on them. Sympathetic magic, they call it."

I looked up to see him giving me that sad smile.

My creation had the face of a blond angel perched on the torso of a tasty bare-chested jock. I sighed. "Does he look like a personal portable wishing well?"

"That's going to get you a boyfriend?" His eyes squinted a moment at the doll, then he shook his head. "We def need to get out."

"It's Tuesday. There's nothing to do."

"Let's go somewhere." He leaned over and made a playful grab at the doll. "You could bring your date along."

"Be serious." Now that I had finished, I felt sorta silly holding it.

"How about getting tattoos?" He lifted up his T-shirt a little, exposing his flat stomach. "I could get some black flames around here." His finger circled his belly button.

"I've got no scoots. I bet your wallet is nearly empty too."

"So piercings are out, then."

I gathered up all the excess pieces that had fallen on the floor into a small neat pile. It looked like the scrapped photos from some weird manikin shop. "My mom won't let me pierce anything but my ear."

"Maybe you need to get something pierced that she won't see." He smirked.

"Gack. Think not."

Han pulled my pillow under his head. "I know what. Let's check out the Copy Center."

I rolled my eyes. "You mean check out that guy working there."

He smiled, not the least bit ashamed that I had known what he was really after. "Dana told me he's still there."

With Han there's always another "that guy." This one was an ultra-cute boi working the counter. Our little fag-hag friend Dana swore up and down that the guy was gay. Of course, she liked to think that any thin little boy who used a lot of gel in his hair and had more than one piercing in each ear was queer. Her track record was pretty damn good though; she figured out us.

"C'mon, c'mon, let's go. Just come out there with me." His voice was nearing a whine, which was the last thing I wanted to hear on a dull night.

But I never could say no to him, which was probably another reason he liked to hang with me. "All right."

"You're not bringing that along?"

Actually, I hadn't been thinking of bringing the paper doll. It was just still in my hand, forgotten, as I reached for my fleece vest on the chair. But the tone in his voice, so queenly sarcastic, made me want to be contrary. "Yeah, that way when you start flirting with that boy, I won't be lonely."

"So weird." He dashed for the bathroom and spent fifteen minutes making sure his hair and face were perfect. When he came out, he looked the same.

Han wasn't due to get his permit for another six months, so we had to walk or bike everywhere when we couldn't get a ride. Thankfully, my house was not that far from the strip mall where the Copy Center was. Seems like no suburban house in Jersey ever is far from a mall.

The boy at the counter was nice. No doubt. With that certain tint of bleached blond hair all the boys in the city had—the dye box must be labeled Queer #5—swept up over his forehead. He wore a necklace of thick silver links that drooped down on the T-shirt he wore underneath his unbuttoned work shirt. His cheap shiny name badge read Bailey. I turned my head to laugh a little; with that name he never had a chance of being straight.

Han went into action, starting with a grin when they made eye contact. I decided to amuse myself by making some copies of the voodoo doll and went over to the boxy machines by the wall.

I glanced up to see how things were progressing. Han and the counter boy were leaning over the counter, chatting. Han tapped the boy's name tag playfully. It never took him long to hook up.

I made faded versions of my voodoo doll, moving the switch to Utter Light, and a gothic edition with everything pitch-black by reversing. I wasted another fifty cents on expanding the cute parts. Everything went into the recycle bin.

Boredom was quickly setting in.

Han came over just before I succumbed to the temptation to discover what "optional automatic duplexing" would do.

"So?"

He held up a bright yellow Post-It note. On it was written a welcome seven digits, along with an email address. Han wore the smug smile of success. "I think I know what my Friday night will be like."

I tried to look like I could care less, even though I was envious about how easy he made being gay seem.

"C'mon, let's go," I muttered, and started to trudge out of the shop. I heard him follow behind me.

Then came the jingle-jangle of the bells at the front door. I stopped in my tracks. Han bumped into me. He started to speak but then went quiet. Blame the guy who'd just walked into the Copy Center. Too much, just too much.

I fought to keep from staring at him, deciding to turn around and drag Han out with me. And maybe take a peek back at him just before the door.

Han, though, I saw, was already following the guy's every move with his eyes as he walked by. My friend almost smacked his lips in hunger. "Look at that," he whispered to me. "Bet his screen name doesn't have 'boy' in it."

I nodded, lost in admiring thought. The guy wasn't that much older than us, but def he was no teen.

Han started towards him, but I reached out and grabbed his arm. "What are you doing?" I hissed.

He looked at me and smiled, trying to seem helpless. The same look he gave whenever he ditched me to go talk with some new boy. "But he's so damn hot," he whined softly in my ear.

"But you just got Counter Boy's number," I said with a tip of my head towards Bailey.

Then he said it. In a voice that seemed almost innocent in its eager-puppy happiness. "There's always one more."

Both Bailey and I watched Han walk over to where the guy stood at the copy machines. I wish I hadn't seen Counter Boy's reaction. It made my stomach, maybe even my heart, sink when he went all pale and then tore up a little piece of paper in his hands.

Then I saw the guy lift up the lid to the copier—and find my doll. I had forgotten all about the thing. How stupid! I wanted the floor to rip open and swallow me up. No such luck. I blushed and looked away and quickly found that worse and had to look back.

He was showing the paper doll to Han, who smirked and pointed over at me. Again I had to blush and turn away, feeling more embarrassed than humanly possible. I didn't dare look back. Bad enough Han was landing another. This guy knew me for the silly kid I really was.

"Excuse me" came over my shoulder.

He was there, standing next to me, holding out my voodoo doll. "I think you left this in the machine." He smiled at me, not the sort of grin you give some dumb kid to share in the awkwardness of the moment, but the sort where you truly are smiling at him—at me, I mean. I felt suddenly warm and, yeah, tingly all over.

"Thanks" was all I could manage to say. As I took the flimsy thing from him, I couldn't help but notice some weird connection... idea... I'm not sure. It's just that I was aware that my doll had blond hair and blue eyes and so did he. Not the store-bought kind, but the real deal. So what, though, right? I mean, millions of others do too. But he also had the same trim but hottie build, and his sand-washed blue jeans were close to the same color as the turquoise of the doll's swim trunks.

"He's cute."

That startled me—I had been staring at the guy's dimples—and for a moment I had the awful sinking feeling that he was talking about Han. But his eyes never left me. The doll again.

"Thanks." I inwardly groaned at my high vocab.

I risked a glance over the guy's shoulder and saw that a dejected Han had made his way back to the counter but Bailey was ignoring him.

"This is going to sound weird, but just a few blocks from here there's this awesome coffee house and... well, do you like coffee?"

I didn't know what to say—I wasn't even sure right then whether I did like coffee, but the last thing I wanted was to hesitate, so I quickly nodded and stammered out a "Yeah, sure." When was the last time I'd had a cup of coffee?

"Great." He smiled again and everything inside me went warm. I almost giggled.

He opened the door for me and I barely remembered to wave "see ya" to Han, who stood there, his mouth both open and pouting. I had never seen him wear that expression before.

That made me chuckle a little. The guy told me his name was Cameron, which is a sexy not silly gay name. He led me through the parking lot to his Jeep. A Jeep! To my mind, that meant he was fun— at least, that's how I always pictured boys that drove them. Especially when they had the top down in autumn.

The wind was strong. He pulled out fast and showy, driving wild, and I laughed at the speed. The doll flew out of my hands. I honestly didn't care.

THE
RESURRECTIONIST

YOUNG WALLACE COULD NOT FIND COMFORT IN his books that bleak afternoon. The family house was overrun with mourners, and the thin walls did not shield his bedroom from their idle chatter. He still wore the black wool the early morning funeral had demanded, though his jacket hung in the wardrobe.

He closed the volume in his lap. The title lettering, *Easing the Blood*, was worn, the edges of the cloth binding a little battered. His father had bought the book at a second-hand store on a recent business trip to London.

Wallace closed his eyes and rested his head against the back of the old chair he sat in. Images and thoughts of the American Mitchell's rest cures for treatment of nerves and hysterics floated around in Wallace's mind. Seclusion, yes that was one element of the cures, and that sounded fine right about then.

The squeak of the door hinges broke any attempt of his to find a moment's solace. He lightly lifted his eyelids to see his mother standing in the doorway. The faint smell of lavender, her favorite, drifted into the room.

"Yes, Mother?"

"Wallace, won't you come down?" A black linen handkerchief

twisted in her hands.

"To what end? Father would not want his son to shed any tears. Not that Uncle Heath deserved them."

"Shame on you. Your uncle loved this family."

"He was your uncle, Mother. And if coming to dinner every odd Sunday to share a cigar and his views on the Continent are signs of love, well I suppose he adored us."

Wallace was intrigued when his mother's face actually went a shade paler than he thought possible for a grieving woman.

"Do not think such caddish behavior will release you from tonight's watch."

"On the contrary, I think being out in a bone-yard," he said the rakish word with a thin grin, "might be desirable to a house full of distant relatives lying about their fondness for the departed."

Her eyes narrowed. "What is worse for you, Wallace? Needing to hate your family or needing to be alone?" She slammed the door behind her.

He would have thrown the book across the room, hoping she would have heard the sound of it striking a wall. But that would have been foolish; he doubted the volume would have survived the impact, and then his floor would have been littered with pages of tiny words and drawings.

The carriage driver managed to find every missing patch of cobblestone along the ride to the cemetery. Wallace worried that the next jounce would trigger the old service pistol resting in the bag at his side. His father had insisted in very loud terms that he bring it along for protection. The thought of shooting anyone made him queasy. He had read about the damage a bullet can inflict on a man. But then, maybe it was the ill effects of the ride that churned his stomach.

When they arrived outside the gates, Wallace stepped out of the cab. The Manchester night held a damp chill that permeated even the thick coat he wore. He looked back to the distant gaslights of the city, but they were nothing more than yellow wisps on the horizon.

Wallace reached up and paid the driver what he deserved and not a penny more.

He barely understood the man's muffled curses beneath the woolen comforter wrapped around the driver's neck.

The cemetery gates were towering, crafted of black wrought iron, and if they attempted to offer hope with reliefs of angels, the atmosphere of that night dispelled the endeavor. A gap of several inches spread between the gates, and he pushed through and into the grounds of the cemetery.

Thin streams of fog drifted about the ground. Wallace made his way along the path, guided by his memory of the morning burial. He went over a hill and saw a glow in the distance and headed towards it.

A lantern illuminated the tired features of Durben, the family retainer, as he sat on a blanket lying besides the fresh-turned earth of Uncle Heath's grave. The man looked ready for game shooting, with his warm clothes and the rifle that rested in his lap.

"Master Wallace." He gave the lad a nod and a tip of his cap as he rose to his feet.

"Has it been quiet?"

"Aye, perhaps sack 'em up men don't care for an old hide."

Durben's reference to the graverobbers plaguing Manchester was not lost on Wallace. He silently cursed that the family considered a metal grate around the coffin in poor taste. Instead they would rather bother the men to keep watch so the remains were secure from theft..

Wallace reached into his pocket for the coins that father had given to pay for the cab ride. He tossed a threepence to Durben. "A man shouldn't go to his bed with a dry throat on such a night. A bit of gin will keep away vapors."

Durben caught the coin easily. "Did you read that in one of your books, young master? If so, the writer's to my liking."

Wallace shrugged. "Perhaps."

"Be well, sir." And Durben began to whistle a tune, something jaunty Wallace didn't recognize, and headed back to the gates and to town.

Wallace settled down on the blanket, near the warm light of the lantern. He took out a bell from the satchel to ring if someone intruded—hopefully the watch would come—and a book he had taken from his father's library. The pistol remained in the bag.

Wallace was lost in thought, considering a line from the page under his fingertips—*That old-somebody I know, / Greyer and older than my grandfather, / To give me the same treat he gave last week*—when his nose itched at the sudden scent of rose water in the air.

He glanced about and saw the woman coming near. Her head and shoulders were covered with a dark shawl. Much effort had been done with a needle and thread to hold together her green dress and keep a semblance of femininity.

When she was only a few feet away she lifted off the shawl from her head. Her hair was long and dark, much more luxurious-looking than the rest of her. She seemed surprised to see him sitting there.

"It's well past the hour to pay respects." Wallace moved his hand near to the bell.

She nodded and brought a finger up to the corner of her eye, as if to staunch a tear. "I knows, good sir." Her accent sounded of the streets. "But I han't said farewell."

"The funeral was this morning," Wallace replied.

"I thoughts it best to come when the family was gone."

"Oh?"

Again she nodded and took a step closer to the grave. Her shoes were badly scuffed. "The deceased and I," she blushed suddenly and looked down at the dark patch of ground. "The family din't know."

That was the last statement from her that Wallace expected. He trembled suddenly and brought a hand up to his mouth to stifle a gasp. "Really," he said in a low tone after needing a moment to recover.

She looked at him and the blush on her cheeks swiftly turned to a blanche. "Yer family? I han't known." She picked up the edges of her dress and stepped back, revealing several inches of the smooth expanse of her legs.

"Wait." He motioned with his other hand for her to stay. "I am far harder to offend than the rest."

She smiled and sat down next to him on the blanket. "It's a cold night. I'm thankful for yer lantern."

"The light and heat are free."

"Ain't it odd for a young boy to spend the night in a bone-yard?"

He laughed a single note, strong and bitter. "I have not been a boy for several years."

She looked confused at his response. Her eyes fell upon the book in his lap. She reached over and closed it to read the cover. "Dramatic Romances? Yer a romantic?" Her hand stayed on the book, her arm lightly laying over his leg and groin.

"Far from it. That is why I read such treacle, in the hopes that something in me will thaw."

She chuckled, though he did not see the joke, until she brought her hand off the book and onto the uppermost region of his thigh and said, "It takes a warm hand to make some things thaw." Her grip moved a bit to the right and squeezed.

He reached out and took a gentle hold of her by the chin, pulling her face an inch closer. She closed her eyes and pursed her lips ready for a kiss, but Wallace merely looked over her face. When after several moments she had felt not the warmth of his lips, she opened her eyes. He gave her his best sneer. "My dear uncle, the now so freshly departed, touched me down there with far more élan than you."

Her expression abruptly changed to that of disgust. "Yer a damn bastard," she spit at him.

Wallace watched as she stumbled while trying to stand. The sound of her dress ripping as her foot stepped on the hem was loud. She rushed off, probably in the direction she had come, that of the front gates.

He brushed his nose with the back of his palm, the cloying stench of her cheap perfume still lingered in the air. Ugh, to think if she had only been an hour or so earlier, he might have accidentally caught her rutting with old Durben. That would have been an uncomfortable sight.

Wallace shook his head. He was eager to return to the poetry when the faintest of sounds met his ears. He stood utterly still, wondering what he heard. A scritch-scratch again and again. Not the step of the woman; he doubted she would be back. Probably looking for easier purses to swindle.

Now that he was affording the odd sound attention, it seemed to expand for his ears, becoming almost a medley. Still that harsh scuffing, but there had begun a thudding and even some distant note he couldn't quite fathom. It was almost as if the sounds were coming from below him. Curiosity drove Wallace to cautiously crawl over to the fresh grave-mound. The clamor grew a tad clearer, and Wallace's ears discerned a weak "Help."

He rolled onto his back, fingers idly digging at the soil. A part of him wondered what kind of monster remained so calm, so even of breath knowing what he knew? He pushed such thoughts aside for the moment and let his memory turn back to a book from his room, the one on the shelf next to the copy of Vathek. A slender volume with red calfskin binding smooth from so much handling: *Accounts of the History of the Great Plague in London*. Back in 1665, with the constant fear of falling victim to the Black Death, bodies were hastily buried. When the crypts and mausoleums were opened to receive the next lot, they would often find some caskets with lids askew, the wood marred with deep scratches, and some of the corpses had bitemarks along their arms and legs. Witnesses to such grisly discoveries claimed that the poor souls had not been dead when interred and they had awoken from some thanatologic state and found themselves trapped and surrounded by death. In their madness to get out they often resorted to autophagy. Wallace had always thought such accounts so ridiculous as to be amusing. Rats and rot were no doubt to blame.

But he was willing to suspend his disbelief thanks to the cries and struggles of his uncle beneath him.

Could the man hear him? Should he call out, let poor Uncle Heath know who sat only a few feet atop him? Wallace found the irony so sweet to mentally digest that he grinned like a child enjoying a sweetmeat, savoring the flavor, turning it over again and again in his thoughts.

Poor Uncle. Not to have awakened beforehand at the physician's touch. To not wake during that horrible day spent lying in the back room of the house waiting for the funeral arrangements. To not stir and spook the horses while the carriage made its way to the boneyard. At any of these instances, he might have been saved, but no, Fate was cruel to one and kind to another. Right then, Wallace thought Her very kind indeed.

The unmistakable sound of something plunging into the soil broke Wallace's first jovial thoughts in years. Not five feet away stood an ugly man wrapped in a dirt-encrusted overcoat. He leaned on an old spade. Around a leer of crooked teeth in an unshaven jawline he spoke. "So, a cony we has 'ere." The voice was harsh and thick with phlegm.

Wallace stood up, startled. He went for the bell, but before he could grasp the handle, another hand took it from the blanket.

"None of that." The woman from earlier brought the bell to her bosom. Her eyes were wide with excitement as they darted between the man and Wallace.

"Go on, run off, get yer constable. Won't matter. The bloke's comin' with us." The man pulled the spade out of the ground and began advancing.

Resurrectionists! How stupid of him, thinking the tart was only a petty thief when her trade was far more larcenous. She had been the failed lure. But the coin paid by anatomists was, no doubt, far too pretty to their ilk to let a body slip away.

He should run. Wallace had no illusion as to their kindness. Harm would come if he remained. But he still heard the sounds of his uncle beneath the fresh grave. What would happen when they started digging? Would they be so startled, so horrified by the cries that they fled, leaving the old man to eventually expire? Or might they fathom what had happened and decide that families that inter in this yard would be generous for returning fallen kin? He could imagine them bringing back a sickly but very much alive Heath, back to the house so that me might recover. Then one future night, Wallace would hear the door creak open and know that his dear uncle wanted to express his affections once again.

He shuddered. He could not take that chance.

He nodded quite obviously to the rogues and bent down to pick up the satchel, beginning to walk off in the direction he surmised the gates lay. The laughter at his back, high and stinging from the woman, low and weak from the man, made reaching into the bag and finding the handle of the revolver far easier.

When Wallace turned around bearing the firearm, the two stood besides the grave, the man with the shovel ready to bite down into the earth, the tart holding up the lantern. Wallace could still hear his uncle, scratching with bloody hands at the lid of the coffin, screaming out for release, and he was shocked that the resurrectionists had not yet taken heed.

The freshly-oiled trigger moved with his finger. The sound of the shot was nothing compared to the man's cry at having his shoulder explode in a rain of blood and bone or the woman's scream of shock and horror. The rogue toppled, like a child's toy, falling onto the mound, trying to turn over and clutch his wound. She dropped the bell, causing it to dimly chime as it hit the ground. Wallace winced, hoping that the watch had not heard the sound of the bell, not wanting anyone else to come and intrude on a family matter.

Wallace took a few steps closer and aimed the revolver at the tart. She had tripped on her long dress again and crawled over the dirt trying to get away. "P-please," she begged, her face wet with tears.

"Did you not hear him?" Wallace's eyes glanced in the direction of the mound, looking right through the wounded man.

She shook her head as if she didn't understand him. He did not even feel the second pull of the trigger, did not hear the shot. Only realized the woman was dead when the blood on her face dripped down her cheeks in the same path as her tears had run. He then finished off the man.

Wallace went back to the blanket. The end of the revolver burned his knee when he rested it there, but it mattered little. When his father came in the morning to relieve his watch, he would head home and have salve applied. There was no sense leaving, not when he had several more hours left before the cries of his uncle died off to a satisfying silence.

PATH OF
CORRUPTION

LET'S START WITH THE TRUTH: I FOLLOWED HIM. There, now I can set the tone. Not that I usually stalk people, but he was different.

So I waited outside the shop, peering into the windows as if browsing from the street, but I was watching him. That he was actually buying something surprised me. He did not look the sort to frequent a gallery, especially that establishment. Were weird masks his taste? The ones on display, crafted from tooled leather and animal bones and graced with burlap wings struck me as truly macabre. I almost walked away, leaving the empty stares of raccoon or perhaps possum skulls perched on calfskin.

Yet I was held fast. When he left the store—without pausing to offer me even a glance—I stood there, breathing in his smell. One more inhalation and a minute's passing happened before I followed again. I never expected to earn his attention but rather let my eyes follow the length of his pretty frame with supposed little risk.

He led me down to Jackson Square; the weekend filled it with tourists and regulars, the artists displaying their paintings and caricatures along the wrought iron fence binding the park. In my two years of living in the Crescent City, I had never seen anyone walk that park.

A snack at L'Madeline's seemed his goal. Outside, I sat down on a metal bench and waited. Resting and inert, I felt little the predator. More embarrassed for acting in such a ridiculous fashion. After years of keeping a secret so well, I could not easily bring myself to reveal the truth of my desires for another man.

So I wondered why this boy had lured me into stalking him. My first glimpse was on a side street to Royal. He was vastly different from the other young men walking the French Quarter. Slender and pale, with almost platinum-colored hair that hung loosely down his neck. His dark sunglasses and worn clothes lent the impression he was a night dweller that had crept out for some reason to take a glimpse of the sun.

He left the cafe to walk down the alleys that led back to Bourbon Street—the infamous thoroughfare of the Quarter, but truthfully a disappointment during the day. Those walkways had the rare person traveling besides us, but still I followed, my mind often urging me to turn back but never quite vehement enough that I listened. I wondered why he did not turn around and confront me. My footfalls were neither quiet nor calm. Perhaps he simply chose to ignore my existence. No matter, I was saved when he left the known parts of Bourbon. He passed the Line.

Newcomers to the Quarter hear of the Line if they spend any serious time downtown. Eventually the tourist trappings fall aside, the restaurants fade back, and you are only left with gloomy looking buildings. Most are bars of ill repute squatting down ready to gorge themselves on sodden customers. From the few fellow grad students I occasionally socialized with, I learned that beyond the almost visible line were places a normal guy, a straight decent fellow, just should not go. Gay bars, rough spots, leather dens, areas where your ass either got shoveled or kicked in. And though the warnings were taboo entreaties, I had not the courage to cross.

So I watched him go with a sigh of regret. He never looked back, and neither did I. And the walk back to the streetcar stop seemed bland by comparison.

SOMEWHERE I HEARD THAT NEW ORLEANS HAS two different patron gods, each presiding not over different parts of the city but rather the times. During the day, it is the sly Mercantile, the one who stands grinning behind the counter. He may be met as a sophisticate selling artwork or antiques, or be the street dealer with lewd T-shirts and garish Mardi Gras posters. But he will try to sell you something, anything, name your price.

But at night, New Orleans becomes the domain of the Truck Driver, an avatar cruel and crude, laughing while he spills his beer on your sleeve, promising to show you sights never seen before, but all guaranteed to arouse. His language is blunt and to the point. The Mercantile wants your business, thrives on it. The Truck Driver couldn't care less, because he knows you have come to watch and don't feel like going home early. Or hungry.

Since I like to think of myself as somewhat sophisticated if not downright neurotic, I often avoided offering myself to the Truck Driver. At night most of the French Quarter is alive and crawling down Canal and Bourbon, with the other streets asleep except for the rare insomniac. And normally I am of little mood for drunken crowds. I'd rather lose myself in a book back at the dorm. But one night late this past semester I sought refuge in their madness; for three weeks I had been barraged with papers and tests, and the notion of just once losing myself seemed like medicine. Come morning, should I regret something, well that was a New Orleans tradition, too.

I had come down on the streetcar with friends, letting them act as faulty guides and chaperons. With a beer clutched in hand, and my college sweatshirt on as a warning label to the locals, I was ready to drink deeply that night. All was fine, even the two hours spent in the strip joint. I enjoyed the rank smell of sweat and smoke more than the dancers, who seemed too eager to leave the stage; their social security checks must have been waiting for them in the back. But I was a consummate actor, in part thanks to the no-cover-charge-but-necessary-three-drink-minimum rule, and my friends never saw my disinterest in flouncing breasts.

Outside the club, I took a moment to clear my head. The brick walls here are great for this. One can lean against them and feel the world coming back into focus. Perhaps I should suggest that a bit of powdered brick added to chicory coffee might serve as a hangover remedy. My renewed perception let me spot him down the street. The clothing was so similar, perhaps a different shirt, that I wondered if I wasn't having some weird Dixie-beer induced flashback. But no, through the passing mob my eyes were teased with him standing in front of a trader's shop, one arm casually draped around the cast-iron horse heads, relics from when busy folk had to tie up their steeds.

I rapped my head against the wall ever so slightly, letting my fellows chuckle at the display. I felt trapped. Leaving them would only invite questions, none of which I could readily answer. But the desire to go to him was demanding, making me reckless. My mind on a rampage, I muttered something about getting a refill and wandered into the crowd. I prayed they would not follow as I waded past the doomsayers, who smelled rank like bad bologna stuck between their sandwich board signs. When I could no longer see my fellows and my last link to school and sanity was gone, I headed directly towards him.

This time his eyes were on me, casually, as I approached. I nearly lost my nerve, but to have come so close and then break away would be too disheartening. So we met besides the black horse head with its rust showing underneath the paint. Never having been so close to him, I was surprised at his young age. But his confident pose had not a measure of inexperience. Since I did not yet have the strength to stare him straight in that delicate face, I found myself staring at his long fingers idly stroking the post's huge nostrils.

"Whew, it's good to get out of that crowd. Felt like I was going to be swept along the street." My voice had a nervous edge to it, making me cringe slightly when I finished.

He shrugged. "Nights here are like that." He had a soft voice, barely above a whisper. "Surprised to see you here, thought you were more of a day walker."

The remark was received and noted. So he had known I followed him that day. "Yeah, but something brought me out tonight. You seem to blend in here."

"That's not a compliment." He flashed me a grin.

"Are you waiting for anyone?" Hope nipped at my fingers, ready to flee if he should answer yes, someone else, someone better looking, perhaps taller or bigger.

"Sort of, but seeing as you're here, guess I might not have to."

That left me confused, but I nodded, feeling it the right thing to do. "Umm, you want to go somewhere and get a drink and talk?"

"Sure, I know a place."

I followed him as we made our way along the sidewalk, avoiding the packed street to make faster time. I dreaded that one of my school chums would catch sight of me and kept my eyes trained on his backside, which was not all together a bad sight. Before I knew it, the crowd had thinned out to mere stragglers. We had reached that damned Line.

He crossed it with ease, then turned around. I hesitated only a moment, realizing that it was too late to turn back. It was almost shameful how uneventful crossing over into unfamiliar territory actually felt.

Farther down the street, we reached a small doorway. Beyond, the room was dark, with dim splotches of light from weak bulbs hanging in the rafters. Small tables and chairs were placed haphazardly about though several people sat close together on the floor amid throw pillows. The bar was low, with too many bartenders milling about, fighting over the odd customer who wanted something to drink. A dim chord of music hung in the air, supplied by an unseen guitar. It was mournfully apparent that conversation, offers and promises, perhaps even deals of flesh were the draw. What was the minimum here, I had to wonder.

We sat at one of the few empty tables. It was odd how such a quiet place could be so crowded; amid all the whispering, mouths barely moved. And I was disappointed that all sorts of couples sat down with their drinks; I had expected, had even hoped for, something more blatantly gay as a site for my initiation.

Drinks were set before us; there was no choosing apparently. I took a sip from the wet glass and found it bitter but strong. He seemed relaxed as ever, just content to stare at me it seemed, yet such a demeanor I decided to be a carefully constructed wall. In a subdued voice, I started the conversation. "My name's Preston." Offering my hand seemed childish and utterly inappropriate for what I was hoping would happen that night.

He took more than a moment to respond. "Brandon."

My hand shook the glass a little, but I cast my eyes about the room to avoid dwelling upon it. "An interesting place. Never saw anything like it before. Almost Bohemian."

He made a slight smirk. "A lot of the hustlers take johns here to settle terms before going farther. And then there are a number of places nearby to go. Haitian cabby drifts about like a checkered shark in case its a hotel job."

I took a hearty gulp of the drink after that. As my throat burned, the truth crashed down taking everything apart like a dropped puzzle. I may have had an innocent life up to then, but never had I thought myself naive. Where to look? The table, the floor, my arms, all covered with fragments of my fantasies. Odd that he was clean.

"Don't tell me you didn't know." He playfully rolled his glass between those pale hands. "You approached me, were tracking me the other day."

I was still in shock, my mouth no doubt open. I came to when I heard "Enough of this," and he rose to leave. My arm shot forth and grabbed a hold of his hand. His skin felt cold and clammy, and my first instinct was to let go and rub warmth back into my fingers.

"No. Please stay. It's all right with me. Really."

He sat back down, but still I could feel that more bricks and mortar had been added to whatever wall separated us. I yearned to knock it down before sharing anything with him, but realized that sitting between us was the Truck Driver, squinting and hooting, offering to pull away Brandon's shirt to let me see a little skin before I paid the bill.

On such new ground, with no maps or guides, I had but one recourse. To feel my way around him and hope to find some crevice that would let me slip inside.

"What are... what are your rates?"

"Depends on what your needs are." He leaned closer, reaching across the small table so that his fingers brushed against the hand that held my drink. That touch made me shiver, not only from the erotic jolt that traveled my skin, but also the dank nature, as if his temperature worked on a different scale than mine.

I timidly wrapped his fingers with mine, choosing to disbelieve the damp chill I felt. The words tasted as bitter as the drink, but had to come out. "I want... I want to sleep with you. Spend the night. Maybe the morning." I quickly finished off my drink.

The smirk was back in full force, making his face look almost bestial. "Not just sleep... "

He enjoyed making me squirm with the request. Damn, I wanted the waitress to bring me another glass so that I might speak more, but now the bar looked empty, the guitar sounded too loud. My mouth was open but only small, guttural sounds came out. I think I trembled; perhaps a few drops of sweat fell onto the table.

I forgot that my hand was still over his until he squeezed my fingers. "No problem, I see what you need. Pay for the drinks and let's get going."

My open wallet was a siren call. At least two waitresses showed at the table, each eyeing the other balefully over the bill. No words were said, so I threw down a twenty to leave them fighting over the paper. Brandon leaned against the doorway waiting for me. Now that an arrangement had been made—though I did not recall a price even mentioned—his stance had changed. Before his slim build seemed ready to quiver if not twist and dance about. Each step was made with wild abandon. Now his hips were cocked like a gun, his tread more slow. He languished about, his arms spread wide at times to stroke the buildings along his side. I had a nagging hard-on for him, and stuck my hands in my pockets to conceal my interest. He noticed immediately and began to laugh, an oddly loud sound when compared to his soft speech.

We went along a maze of streets and corridors until we came to an inner courtyard, a rare sight most folk who walk the French Quarter never see. Often they contain old fountains or lush gardens. This one was bare except for several crates stacked like precarious towers and a metal gate set before stone steps down one wall. Brandon had one foot on a slim staircase that led to the upper floors of an adjoining building.

I glanced one last time at the odd gate—basements were a rarity in New Orleans. The city was below-sea level, and I was intrigued where those steps led. But Brandon called out my name once, and my raging interest returned to what could happen atop the other flight of stairs.

The upper floor was riddled with rooms. Behind closed doors I could hear sounds and moans, but was unsure if all were sounds of pleasure. I realized now how dangerous my situation was; I had come to an area of the city with no clear way of going home, led by a complete stranger. The urge to run, break away and head back to the safety of my dorm crept over me for a moment. But before it had time to act, I had followed Brandon into one of the rooms.

It was small, mostly cramped space framing a futon and an old chest. A Salem Witchcraft poster hung on one wall, along with a bizarre display of slate shards. The pile of the stones seemed more than haphazard and was disturbing to look at. Other than a few clothes scattered about, the rest was old carpet.

He shut the door behind us and leaned against the wood. I waited for a few minutes in the moonlight that streamed in through a window, feeling somewhat at a loss for words or actions. He just stared at me with those dark eyes. Then he walked to me, stepping so close I could feel his cool breath on my face.

"Take off my clothes." A demand, not a request.

My hands trembled as they went to his shirt. The tips of my fingers brushed against smooth, cool skin as I pulled it off. His chest was slim but toned, nearly snow white except for dark rings around each nipple. I wanted to caress him there, but I know that would not be following whatever rules had to exist in such situations. So his worn jeans were next. As I unzipped them, he stepped closer to me, until our bodies nearly touched. I pushed down the denim to expose a pair of black boxers, the front of which showed the strain of Brandon's erection. I knelt down, dragging along the jeans, passing with admiration firm, muscular legs with not a wisp of hair to be seen.

I helped him out of his sneakers, peeled off his socks, and then the jeans were free. He stood there only in his underwear, which was so dark compared to his skin that it looked like his body stopped at the waist only to begin again in mid-thigh. I was entranced by the contrast, and one of my fingers had to reach out and touch his boxers just to ensure that it was indeed fabric. My hand ended up close to the inner side of his leg, and I began to lazily stroke skin as smooth as milk.

I looked up to see a half-smile on Brandon's face. I could accept that. I came closer until we were brushing against each other. My own erection was still constrained, reminding me that I was still fully dressed.

Then one of his hands went to my neck, cupping underneath my chin. To my flushed skin, it was a cool compress. I sucked in my breath, feeling the blood race around his touch. Then, that hand drifted down, over my shirt, to my waist. It hesitated a moment before sliding up between the fabric and my skin.

That I could feel such pleasure in his stroking my chest was astounding, I feared that I would completely collapse into a quivering mass if and when his hand went lower. I could not help but sigh and softly moan. My eyes closed.

He never said a word as his hand left me. The loss of such contact was frightening; all of a sudden I was left disoriented. I opened one eye to see that he was stretched out on the futon, one hand stroking the front of his boxers. The other did a slow wave to bring me closer.

That I would have to undress myself was a disappointment. I saw again how immense and intact that wall of Brandon's remained. For the last few minutes, I had been lost in fantasy. The fact that I was paying for a night's passion, however exquisite it may turn out to be, returned and threatened to dull my desire with self-disgust. My hands were fumbled at removing my clothes. If he noticed my inner turmoil, he said nothing to ease my thoughts.

Stripped bare except for my briefs, I crawled onto the futon besides him. He still wore that almost-grin. Along with adrenaline, my blood carried doubt, the whole mixture making me feel weak and lost as I laid there. Then Brandon leaned towards me on one elbow and with his free hand began to brush his fingers through my hair. His touch was so gentle that I felt like I had just sipped a tonic to chase away my fears.

We leaned in to kiss. His mouth was chilled, an ice-water bath, but rather than be disturbing I found the sensation delightful. And wickedly I had to wonder what would it feel like if he went down on me with that cold tongue. I held my breath for as long as I could, letting him explore. My arms went around him, sliding along as they made their way to his back. I gripped him close, desperate to bring him closer to me.

At some point, he was atop me, rubbing his whole body against me, bringing shivers along the length of my spine. Then he rolled over, disengaging himself. Rather than speak, he guided my hand down to his crotch. The nerves along my arm readied themselves for what my touch would find.

I slid his boxers down, exposing his erection. Around the base was a sparse arrangement of silver hair that curved down to his scrotum. I leaned in closer to marvel at the dichotomy: it was both the softest skin and yet felt so hard like an icicle. I left myself rub along the length, now and then gliding down to cup his sack in my palm.

When his hand pressed against the back of my head, inching me closer to his cock, I knew what he wanted me to do. I expected his cock to have a taste, but there was none. Rather a certain firmness that was delightful to fill the depth of my mouth. That and the coolness of Brandon's flesh. I wanted to warm him with my breath and throat.

I had no idea if I pleased him; Brandon just lay there calm, looking down at me as I slipped my lips again and again over him.

Finally, he lifted my face from his crotch. I moved slowly, soon realizing that Brandon had managed to slide behind me and that I now faced the mattress. Moments later I gasped as something cold thrust inside of me then quickly withdrew. As the movement returned again and again, I was drawn into heaving breaths while a tide of pleasure and pain ebbed and ripped through me. I could not help but collapse forward and hug the edges of the futon. I heard his laughter.

How long I lasted is beyond me. With a massive moan, I came into the folds of the sheets below me. Soon after, he pulled out from me, then turned me over to watch as he jerked off. His semen sprayed all over his chest and groin, and I was held enthralled by the sight. Then as his labored breathing eased, he dipped a finger into the streaks of cum and he held it up it to my face as an offering. I hesitated, and found him pressing it closer to my shut lips. I opened and took his finger in, tasting him deeply, feeling his salty seed lay on my tongue.

We then slept together. Come morning, instead of a shared kiss, he made me go down on him again. I did so without complaint. Then

I gave him whatever money I had left in my wallet, leaving me only enough change for the streetcar ride back home. He led me back through the streets until we came to a part of Bourbon I recognized. I said good-bye. He merely nodded.

If only that had been enough. Seemed that all my time was spent in remembrance of that night. Perhaps I should have been disgusted, for to some I was merely used. But I did not feel so. Rather my attraction to Brandon had grown beyond the physical. I wanted to meet the challenge of piercing his wall, to find and love the true teen that lurked inside. Are most defrocked virgins so naive?

So the very next night I returned to Bourbon Street to find him. Now that I knew what sort of person I dealt with, the hunt was easier. He greeted me with only a smirk, but this time, when we were inside the brothel, he held onto my hand, guiding me back to the room.

And so for the next two weeks it went, rarely did I fail to find him, once even chasing away another potential customer, though Brandon seemed little bothered by the loss. My studies suffered as the task of college paled in comparison to the challenge of finding love with my prostitute.

My newfound dedication was paying off though. Brandon must have developed a fondness for me to often refuse money in the morning. When he took it, it was half-hearted born of a need. Even the sex became less demanding, allowing me to slow down each caress and find time to savor his taste and touch.

The next step was far too easy, and I found myself staying with him each night, together roaming the streets where he would show me parts of the city few had ever seen. The wall was crumbling; I could hear bits of masonry fall as he guided me about, holding my hand during these private tours of decayed courtyards and manses.

During the day we mostly slept, venturing out only when bored. I abandoned most of my belongings back in my dorm room, taking only the essentials. The only way to embrace him was to turn my back upon the old life and walk a new path.

There were moments I worried that I was chasing after the impossible. Was I only a diversion in Brandon's life, one that would last only so many nights before apathy set in? I often drowned my concerns in bitter drink and his heady presence.

Now the night dweller, I was introduced to the other boys who lived in the building. Like some secret clan, they all spoke in whispers, each I saw with walls holding back their true selves. All were hustlers, though some I think catered to more exotic clientele. At first I found them distant towards me, like I was only a shadow amongst them. Soon, as they saw how much time Brandon and I shared, they began to speak to me, confide in me the events in their lives. I wanted so easily to let my guard down and regard them as friends, but no, there still existed a bit of that wall of my own. The story of Remus was fresh from my studies.

Then one cloud-covered night, with the threat of rain driving most from the open street, Brandon led me not to the room to spend one more night in each other's heat, but to the building's courtyard. He was quiet, the only snatches of conversation he uttered sounded both vague and unsettling. Something was going to happen that night, besides the thick showers that so-often befell New Orleans. I had begun to believe that this would be my last night with him, that tomorrow he would tell me to return to my old ways, to sunlight and textbooks. And loneliness.

The courtyard looked different when lit by fire. All the boys stood about, many of them carrying hand-made torches. I counted several faces hidden behind a variety of sordid masks. Here, one crafted from broken porcelain, there a leather bondage visage complete with zippered eyebrows and lips. One of the boys brought Brandon the elaborate scrolled mask he had bought so long ago. He brushed aside my attempt to help adjust the straps at the back. Now I could physically see his wall rearing up to prevent me from reaching in. The brickwork was far older than the flesh it contained.

A deep groaning of tortured metal sounded as the iron gate was unlocked and thrust wide open. A procession began to climb down the steps. Brandon need not have pushed me ahead of him; I wanted to go down and see the one aspect of his life that had remained hidden from me.

The descent was rough on my senses. Flickering torchlight revealed only dripping stone walls decorated with patches of repellent fungus. The boys remained silent; only the crackling of the fires and the sound of our feet falling upon the tiles reached my ears. The stench of musty earth was thick in the cool air.

How long we walked down those steps I could not guess, but finally, when we reached bottom, my teeth chattered against the cold, and I dreaded brushing against the stonework around me. I followed the others, careful to still feel Brandon's presence behind me. I believe we passed a few unlit chambers, all looking archaic and unsafe to venture in. Someone from the lead of the procession had begun to hum a strange tune that rose and fell in time to our feet. Other voices were added, and I fear to say that some of the whispers emanated from those dark rooms.

The corridor ended in a large circular chamber, and the line of masked and unmasked wound its way around a huge pit set in the floor's center. In the dim light, I could just make out the remains of mosaic tiles surrounding the hole. But if they were decorated with words or icons, I was unfamiliar with any. Though I could hear wind whistling up from the mouth, it looked more like a pool of black water than any depth.

A voice close to me ripped the silence. "Ia Nyogtha! Erikthnar l'hor kadishtu... Ia Nyogtha! Ygnaiih Nyogtha k'yarnak!"

I was horrified to see Brandon's mouth set below the mask, those lips that I had spent so much time touching with every part of my being, now twisted to spit out obscene sounding words. His voice was no longer a whisper, but the hoarse screams of some dying animal pleading for release. Others took up the chant, hurling it from one to another, until the last shouted it down to the pit. Shards of slate were tossed down the pit, making no noise, meeting silently with whatever lurked there.

And that something that dwelled in the darkness of the chasm responded to the entreaties. I could swear that above their hoarse shrieks I heard a terrible sound, like the lapping of thickened water. Their shouting intensified, they began to leap up and down, shaking their limbs.

One boy held out his hand... and was touched by something from the pit. A stream of blackness, deeper and darker than any my eyes had ever been hindered by issued forth and snaked around that boy's pale wrist. It moved like liquid and sounded like poison.

Then each of the boys began to howl, stripping off whatever

clothes he wore. I watched as they finally freed themselves to now twist and jump, a dance both graceful and horrific. And tentacles of the black thing shot forth to touch their skin, stroke their naked bodies with a lover's touch as they laughed and cavorted. Their firm erections were jolted by the creature's lingering touch, as if it sought out the only heat along their bodies, wanting to bring it close. Several came, showering the blackness with their pale cum, all the while howling with glee.

I had not noticed until now that a few of the boys had brought bags along the descent. From them they dumped animals into the pit, letting the darkness swallow up a grand course meal. I say animals, and resist dwelling on the few things that squirmed and bawled as they fell.

My mind screamed for release, and I ran from the room. Even hunched over in the hallway, my thoughts shrieked, wanting peace and forgetfulness. I trembled and cried, wondering if it would not be best to rip my eyes free and cast them aside for having betrayed the rest of the body.

Before my clawed hands moved close, I heard someone enter the corridor from that accursed room. I looked up to see Brandon standing over me, his mask slightly askew, his naked body glistening with an iridescent slime. Even then lust caught me, my eyes glancing downward to note how rigid he was.

He lifted me up gently, to meet his face. Then I watched as one of his fingers reached down to his chest and brought back a daub of that muck. He held it before my eyes; I could see the oily sheen it had. Then he offered it to my lips. I could read nothing of his thoughts through the mask. But the decision was made, had been back in that bar past the Line weeks ago. Before he had a chance to withdraw the offer, I wrapped my mouth around the finger and sucked hard. The slime tasted acrid and felt like cold slush falling down my throat. But I did not gag or show any signs of suffering. Brandon let me taste his finger for several minutes, and then he withdrew, back to the festival and leaving me alone again in darkness. I slipped down the wall, knowing that something black had entered me, now festering in my gullet. When they brought me back to the surface, Brandon half carried me along. I sank into a deep sleep troubled with images of dripping black water.

I awoke to the little sunlight that crept through the boarded windows. To my side, he still slept, his face serene, so different from the mask he wore. I rose without disturbing him and, dressed only in underwear, took the stairs down to the courtyard.

And here I am. The hours have passed, and I have been staring at the closed gate. What happened last night was no delusion, I am sure, but rather something like a wedding. But now to what am I married to?

The night comes upon me still in this fugue. The air holds a slight breeze warm against my bare skin, and I wonder just how cold my touch is now. Nobody forced this path of corruption I walked down upon me, nor did they place my hands on the metal bars and aim my eyes to those dark steps. I am solely to blame.

But to what end?

A light touch on my shoulder does not startle me. The fingers are assuring. I turn to find Brandon before me, naked in the night. One of my hands he takes in his, guiding it to his bare chest, against the smooth skin. And my touch meets no resistance, nothing to prevent finding his racing heartbeat. We come closer and know that inside we both share a black taint. And together we make our way back to our room. For the first time, I am master upon the bed, selfishly taking before I give any pleasure. And then we lay together and know that for all my waking moments when I dreaded the path I walked, the companion I had found along the way has made the harsh price worth it.

VESPERS

"Puer paruulus oppressus a maiore annum aetatis habens decimum, ebdomadam dierum ieiunet; si consentit, xx diebus."

The Penitential of Cummean

ALL WAS SILENCE. THE MONASTERY CHERISHED quiet above all else, even faith, Brother Saul was sure. Every action was performed in perfectly choreographed silence, from the deliberate touch of the tip of a quill to vellum, to the motioned chewing of simple meals. Whatever prayers were read, were read to oneself and not the rest of the world.

At night, the stillness was thick, enveloping. Brother Saul let it surround him, wore it as he walked the monastery. His destination was the long room where the acolytes slept. They were his charges and he watched over their slumber with an interest that often scared him.

He stood just inside the doorway, holding his breath. Six acolytes slept gently beneath the flimsiest of blankets. All in row. So many bare arms and legs, some coming so close to their neighbors that they nearly intertwined.

"Igor, what the fuck you doing up?" A half-whisper, half-cry, followed by a rude belch and the smell of cheap domestic beer.

Startled, he turned fast and saw Brother Rick leaning up against the old column near the front door of the fraternity house. He was obviously drunk, his sweatshirt stained with the remains of buffalo wings and fifty-cent drafts.

"Oh, damn, you scared me." Saul's mind whirled, thinking of an excuse for being caught up at this late hour staring down at the sleeping pledges. It did not have to be the best of excuses, after all, alcohol had no doubt impaired Brother Rick's deductive abilities. But he wanted to keep things calm, quiet, and get back to his own room fast. "I was on my way to get a drink and heard you climbing the steps."

Brother Rick nodded, the motion exaggerated almost to the point of unbalancing him. "I got to piss." He looked down at the sleeping pledges as if suddenly realizing they were there. He must have forgotten after the second pitcher that it was a Wednesday night when the fraternity forced pledges to sleep on the floor as part of their initiation. "Heh, Igor, think I should give 'em a golden shower?"

Saul cringed at his nickname. They all thought he spent too much time in his room, his 'cave' they called it. But his cell was safe. Even though he had been admiring the row of pledges sleeping in their boxers and briefs, he had kept his pleasure inside. 'Never touch yourself unless in your room' was his consoling maxim.

He left Brother Rick looking for the downstairs bathroom. At the top of the steps, his cell beckoned. Inside were his history books and works in Latin and the hidden sketches of boys and men.

"... and it is safe to say that although the poetic Muses would have preferred a rose garden to the cloister, life in a medieval monastery was as often gay as solemn. The scholarly monks poured over the antique manuscripts every morning - but each afternoon they recited pagan Latin epigrams with their young pupils, and in the

evenings abbot and novice together learned the more
subtle realities of brotherly love."

"The Homosexual Pastoral Tradition"
RICHARD NORTON, 1997

THE SECOND-FLOOR TATTOO PARLOR ON SOUTH Street was his scriptoria, a place of secret pleasure and penance. Below sat a small Cajun grill and on weekend nights the scents from the kitchen drifted up and burned his eyes from whatever they peppered the dishes with. Unobtrusive, the woman, a modern mistress of the biting pen, would always nod when Saul showed her the copies of illuminated manuscripts and tell her what he wanted.

He lay on his stomach, wincing outwardly as she began to ink his back, but inwardly he was tingling with delight. Every time she applied the jewel tones, he could just barely keep from shuddering. This was his flagellation, the whip and leather cord replaced by the needle.

That evening, Saul held up the hand mirror and gazed into the reflection it offered of it's larger mate that hung on the yellowed plaster of the parlor wall. *Odi et Amo* joined the rest of the Latin inscribed onto his back, the lead letters livid in their height and depth, just like a scribe's work.

He was turning himself into a living, illustrated codex, an incunabulum. Oh that sounded so like an incubus that he had to smile. Was there even a difference, he wondered.

An actual medieval jest:

Chronicler: *There once was an abbot renown for his*
skill at healing. A marquess in Burgundy sent for the
cleric for her ailing son. When the abbot arrived it was
too late; the boy had died. He took the boy to a private
room and laid down upon him in the hopes of a miracle.
Nothing happened and the funeral plans were made.

Friend: *The abbot must have been the unhappiest of*
monks. For I have never heard of any monk who lays

down upon a boy whom afterwards did not straightaway
rise up.

BROTHER JERROD'S LITTLE BROTHER SHOWED
up on their doorstep. Unlike the countless abandoned babies that
ended up on monasteries' doorsteps, this was an expected visit. For six
days he was staying at the fraternity while his parents were away on
some trip. Man had been created on the sixth day, Saul recalled.

Billy barely resembled his brother. As if Brother Jerrod, with his
fleshy nose and thick arms, was a crude sketch made before the real
work. The boy was small and delicate; a sixteen-year old sculpture of
taut muscles laid over fine bonework and glimpsed under smooth
skin. His hair was short and dark.

Every time he glanced at the boy, Saul shivered with reverence.

> *"Often, it was said, a man, as he lay in his bed, would*
> *'fall prey to evil thoughts.' Then, in answer, a demon in*
> *the guise of a beautifully sensuous youth would appear*
> *in the man's bedroom where they would engage in 'the*
> *terrible vice.'" There was only one problem. Demons*
> *weren't supposed to have bodies or sperm, so how could*
> *sex happen?*
>
> "The Roots Of Homophobia"
> TERRY BOUGHNER, 1989

THE MONASTERY HAD A BOUNTIFUL POMERIUM,
a sacred open space located just inside the wall. Apple trees grew
abundantly there, and the scent was almost sinful on breezy days in
spring and summer.

With the other monks, Brother Saul worked to gather the apples.
The fruit would be pressed to make cider. He picked the apples by
rote, callused hands briefly feeling over the tender skin, choosing ones
that were just a shade before ripe. Those were his favorites. When he
was confidant none of the others watched, Brother Saul would take

an apple and bite into it, juices running down his chin and sweetness flooding his mouth. Later on he would do penance, remembering the way the fruit lay on his tongue before he swallowed. According to Homer, apples were among the fruits which the accursed Tantalus, imprisoned in Tartarus, could not pluck, the wind ever blowing their boughs away from him.

"Monastic writing on love and friendship in the twelfth century represents some of the earliest evidence we have of the views of homoerotically inclined men."

"The Experience of Homosexuality
in the Middle Ages"
PAUL HALSALL, 1988

'NEVER TOUCH YOURSELF UNLESS IN YOUR ROOM.' He chanted that silently three times when Billy came into the fraternity house den followed by his big brother, who promptly threw his book bag onto the sofa as if staking a claim.

Saul desperately sought to avoid eye contact, but he wanted to stare at the beads of sweat that rolled down the boy's forehead, cheeks, and neck. Billy gave him a nod and cheerfully called out, "Hey Igor." Saul gave him a tired smile. He did feel weak, almost feverish. His dreams, day or night, had become infected with thoughts of the boy.

"For the romance plot with which The Monk opens is not the heterosexual romance plot later depicted with the lurid detail that so scandalized contemporary readers, but a homoerotic one."

"Cloistered Closets: Enlightenment
Pornography, The Confessional State,
Homosexual Persecution and The Monk."
CLARA TUITE,
Romanticism On the Net 8, 1997

"SHIT, THE LAST THING I WANT IS TO SPRING for a motel room."

Saul walked into the kitchen and into a conversation shared between Brother Jerrod and some others. He opened the fridge, took out the milk, and gave the carton a shake. It sounded pitifully empty.

"Dude, that sucks. Maybe you can just blindfold him."

There was a laugh and Brother Jerrod lightly punched the one brother who had freshly earned his cassock after last semester's hazing.

"What's wrong?" Saul asked, eager to turn his attention away from his growling stomach.

"Cindy wants to come over tonight," Brother Jerrod leaned back in his chair. "And Bill's still here."

"Oh." It was all so simple. Another Wednesday, so there was no room downstairs, no empty rooms in the house. Demons do not grant miracles. Saul tried to imagine what to call the blessing he had been given. A boon? An infernal favor?

"He can take my bed tonight."

All of them looked at him with surprise. He was himself shocked how coolly he had spoken. So this was how it felt to be possessed. He decided he enjoyed the sensation, of calm control, of being aware and choosing to ignore consequences.

"Yes, I'll crash on the old recliner. I do it all the time, falling asleep reading."

Brother Jerrod smiled and patted the back of the nearest brother. "Igor, I owe you. This weekend. Steak and Ale."

Because of him my soul is sick,
perplexed and yearning.
His speech upon my heart
is like dew upon a parches land.
Draw me from the pit of destruction
that I go down to Hell

YISHAQ BEN MAR-SAUL
(Lucena, 11th Century)

IN THE OLD CLAW-FOOT TUB, A RELIC FROM THE monastery's previous owner, Brother Saul poured more water over himself. It mildly troubled him that he lacked any proper prayers to say while ritually cleansing. He tried saying *'oculum obscoenum'* over and over, but the words held little poetry despite their meaning: the 'obscene kiss,' a pressing of lips to another's dick or ass. The phrase made him chuckle actually, and he wanted this bath to be solemn.

Though the water was lukewarm—the pipes were awful and never carried enough hot water up to the second floor—he emerged excited. He had a vision of the young oblate, asleep on the bed, perhaps with his face lying on its side, mouth slightly apart with the tongue a hidden treasure. Bare back, the rest hidden by cool sheets. Oblate from *oblatus*, "one offered up." The medieval mind was cunning in its choice of words.

Brother Saul wrapped loose robes around him and lightly tread down the hall back to his small cell. The rest of the monastery was still at this hour. All the others asleep. He had to make sure that whatever happened, it happened in silence. Idly he wrapped the belt to his robes around his palm.

Odi et Amo. I hate and I love.

Never touch yourself unless in your room. Never touch another boy unless in your room.

He shut the door behind him as quietly as possible.

LEFT ALONE

DAVE SAT ON THE EDGE OF THE BOARDWALK AND let the cold wind blow around him. The gusts never touched the sands. He had been waiting for the past couple hours. Around him, the cheap tourist trade shops slept, dark against the gaudy lights of the casinos.

It was all so quiet. That used to panic Dave. Once he had needed strong lyrics with stronger words and themes. But six years alone changes a person. He hadn't repaired the ache he felt at losing Jerrod but built around it, keeping the hole ragged but there. He needed quiet for that.

His pockets always held remnants of their time together. He pulled out a small doll of cheap black cloth. Once it had white thread features, but after so much touching and rubbing and the occasional bit of salty tear the face had worn smooth. Three years ago it had been an impulse gift, just one among many that beautiful Jerrod was always bringing him.

A finger caressed the edges of the small body. The touch brought back that weekend spent with Jerrod in New Orleans, making love in small puddles in the park at night. Then, still muddy, they sat down and pretended everything was calm while sipping chicory coffee at Cafe Dumonde until dawn.

His insides were churning, acid brewing. He looked up and scanned the beach for

anything pale. Without moonlight he'd have to watch carefully or risk missing his boy.

ONE NIGHT NOT LONG AGO, HE TOLD EVERYTHING to this girl sitting next to him at a crappy bar. Somewhere in the shadows early Goth music that no one listened to anymore played. Siouxsie and the Banshees moaned because few cared.

The girl just nodded, her dyed-black bangs falling over a surgically-aligned nose.

Maybe an annual rendezvous with a ghost was nothing new to her. Maybe it wasn't. With her manufactured features she didn't look quite human anymore.

"Why not kill yourself? Just wade into the water? Then you could be with him always."

Dave shook his head a few times, the fourth shot of vodka affecting his base movements. "No, doesn't work like that. I'd just float out to sea and be left alone. Trust me on this, I've asked around." The last was a lie to shut her up; he was just guessing. Truth was, he was afraid.

She undid the clasps on the black metal lunchbox she apparently used as a purse, reaching in for a clunky vial and small paintbrush. "Silver nitrate," she whispered as she painted her mouth. "Burns like hell, but stains the lips." Her half-smile glistened sickly with an odd shade, almost gunmetal gray.

He just stared at the shot glass.

DAVE LEAPT DOWN TO THE SAND DUNE BELOW, ignoring the sign that threatened a thousand dollar fine for walking over the dunes. He tread over the browned grass, leaving fresh impressions in the sand beneath him. Some nights he ached so fiercely for Jerrod that every muscle along his spine would lock and he'd be left crying on the tub floor while scalding water from the showerhead would ease his back.

The wind teased with half-uttered words that almost sounded like his name. But Jerrod's ghost never spoke. He would have begged to hear that soft voice again. Even only a sigh or those wonderful little groans that twisted Jerrod's face during passion.

Hands stuffed in his coat pockets to keep them warm, he started pacing up and down the shore. He'd stay all night if he had too, maybe sleep under the boardwalk; he had done that once before.

His boy always appeared from the corner of the eye. One moment the shoreline was clear, and then a glimpse.

Jerrod waited there, just at the waterline's edge, dressed in whatever Dave wanted him to wear that night. Yesterday, he had seen some boy walking through the city streets in a long coat and so that's what he saw again tonight: the ends flapping in the wind, the collar turned up to protect that smooth neck. Jerrod's black hair caught every gust and was almost lost against the sky.

Dave ran out to him like he did every time, worried that he might not reach him before Jerrod disappeared—as had happened the first time. Too much cheap red wine at dinner. Dave nearly collapsed on the beach, while his boyfriend teased him with a midnight swim. By the time Dave realized he could not see Jerrod in the water, it was too late. He was left alone.

They embraced immediately. Alone on the beach, he pressed close, eager to share his warmth. A small rivulet of water slipped from Jerrod's mouth and down his chin. Dave licked it before a drop could fall. His mouth filled with the savory nature of his late boyfriend. Salty. He tasted like the sea.

CRIES BENEATH
THE PLASTER

JOSEPH DIPPED HIS HANDS ONCE MORE INTO the bucket, enjoying the sticky warmth coating his skin. Even at night the studio captured the late summer heat, and the sweat rolled down his face and bare chest to mingle with the crimson stains on his flesh.

He lifted his gory hands from the bucket and wiped them across the blank face of his latest sculpture, urging ample rivulets to flow between the bony fingers that clawed out from where the sculpture's eyes should have been.

After two hours of painstaking work, he managed to coat the entire piece. After one more cursory glance to make sure that no areas of the white plaster were visible, he wheeled over the two heating lamps, ones he purchased cheaply from a bankrupt salon. With three curved stems, each carrying a fat bulb, they looked like grotesque metal flowers. Joseph tapped the floor switch of each with his foot, and the bulbs erupted in an orange brilliance that would bake in the doctored pig's blood to create Joseph's trademark rust-brown patina.

He picked up the bucket and the towel beside it and left the studio. In the kitchen, he put the bucket onto the lowest shelf of the refrigerator for the next piece and took out the carton of milk. He tilted back his head and opened it over him, letting the cold milk wash over his face. He caught most with his open mouth, but allowed the rest to wash over his soiled chest and neck. Milk and blood, he remembered reading, were the sources of life. And after each piece was finished, he made sure to celebrate with the same toast to the mask hanging on the wall.

A gift from an artist friend living in New Orleans, one handcrafted from porcelain in the shape of a grinning jester's face complete with foolscap tassels. Half of the mask was a slick red, looking wet to the touch. The other side a slate gray and rough as granite. The artist had sculpted his inner side, she had told him, and Joseph often spent time staring at the piece, wondering if he began to tear the flesh from his face, whether his skull would resemble the mask.

He looked back at the studio, his lashes thick with white drops. All celebrating aside, 'Dedipus' was truly not finished. That last touch remained, the one that set him above the other artists of the so-called Art Macabre movement. What had started out as the insane whim of a homeless artist five years ago had grown in attention and style to become desirable pieces that disturbed as much as evoked emotion.

Joseph found his vision channeled to compliment this bizarre, morbid trend. But where some other artists tended only to concentrate on the darker elements of the movement, he embraced a more erotic adaptation. Now this piece was almost finished. Through the sweatpants he wore, he rubbed at his crotch. The last touch, the most thrilling...

He walked to the section of his loft that made up his office. Opening the last drawer of the scarred desk, he pulled from a pile a slick magazine. The cover showed a hand-some, half-naked youth in the act of pulling down his gym shorts, a smile on his face as if to tell the reader how much he enjoyed revealing himself within the pages.

He opened the magazine and paged past the models' revealing pictures until he found the classified section. Several of the ads promising escort services and massages had been X-ed over; his fingers traced down these until they found the next unmarked ad of interest:

HUNK OF MUSCLE
Br/br, 26 yr ex-Marine. Well-cut physique. Endowed
in all areas. $150, worth every penny. Out calls only.
Call Scott (212) 955-0980

JOSEPH ANSWERED THE DOOR, LETTING THE young man inside, all the while appraising him: short with limbs built around a large chest almost out of proportion to the rest of his frame. The stern look the man offered Joseph's gaze, coupled with close-cropped brown hair and block-like facial structure, was nearly intimidating. He wore only enough to emphasis his goods: an open denim jacket, the thinnest of T-shirts, and tight jeans.

Each murmured a few words, forgetting salutations to focus more on procedure and payment. After coming to an agreement, Joseph led the hustler into the bedroom and watched as Scott stripped, noting the fine work of muscles that stood out on his chest and calves as the clothes came off.

He made the first move, coming close to embrace the naked young man, enjoying the sensation of his sweatpants rubbing against another's flesh. He guided the young man to the bed, positioning himself on top.

After exploring Scott's mouth, he took hold of his arms at the wrists and pushed them back towards the brass headboard so as to reveal more of the young man's chest. A sudden cry of pain came harsh from Scott's lips as his forearm brushed against a sharp edge of the brass piping. He easily shook free of Joseph's grip and examined the wound. Not a deep slice; the trickle of blood dripped down onto the sheets.

Joseph did not care for the hard look in the hustler's eyes. "I'm not into that pain shit. If you're planning some S&M, might as well give me twenty and show me the door." He placed a hand on Joseph's shoulder, the grip slowly increasing until painful. "Understand me?"

Joseph smiled and nodded, gently taking up the arm with the cut, and kissing the wound as Scott watched carefully. He then left the bed for the bathroom and returned with a roll of white gauze, which he proceeded to wrap around the forearm. Once finished, the young man's eyes lost most of their glare, and he renewed his kissing of Scott's face and neck, working his way down in time with the young man's increased breathing...

JOSEPH POURED A FINGER OF BOURBON INTO the tumbler and handed the glass over to the hustler. The gauze on the arm that accepted the glass was splotchy red where the cut was.

"Here, let me change that for you."

Scott sipped the alcohol while Joseph changed the dressing, dropping the old gauze onto the counter.

"It's not deep. A day or two, you won't even notice it."

Scott did not comment, instead finishing his drink. He grabbed his jacket and stood besides the door. Joseph nodded his understanding and went into his office where he kept his cash underneath an old plaster face cast. He gave Scott four fifties, opened the door for him, and watched him silently leave.

Joseph was once more alone with his work. And he started to chuckle, breaking out into full laughter moments later. He went to the Formica counter in the kitchen and picked up the bloodied bandage where it lay. He brought it to 'Dedipus' and began to wrap the gauze around the sculpture's neck, making sure that the bloodstains were positioned in the front between the clawing hands. The effect, Joseph's trademark, mirrored a grisly cleric's collar, a cue that this work was more than just Macabre, but his. The artist s-miled, pleased with himself, and, as he headed off to the bed again, this time to sleep, he reminded himself to purchase some film for his camera. His friends at the Gallery Outsider would be the first to want to see pictures of his latest piece.

JOSEPH OPENED THE DOOR AND REACHED FOR the wall switch, turning on the studio's lights to chase away the night that had slipped through the studio's windows while he was out cruising. He threw his jacket on the floor and stepped aside to allow the kid—for he could not have been older than sixteen—to follow him inside.

He walked over to the bar besides the kitchen and began to fix himself a double bourbon sans ice. He had not allowed himself a proper measure of alcohol at the bar, instead concentrating on what youths were available. He looked at the one that he brought home. Slim and pale, a mooncalf. "Andy, right?"

The kid simply nodded, his eyes wide as they took in the whole of his studio.

"Would you like a drink? I don't have any weed."

The kid seemed not to hear him, instead walking over to the tall shape that stood in the center of the studio, its nature hidden underneath a white tarp.

"You can look."

The kid turned to Joseph, as if surprised at being offered such a treat. With a slow and gentle hand he pulled the cloth from the piece, revealing a statue definitely inspired by the feminine, though it had grown warped under Joseph's guiding hands. The arms were too long, and had they not been stretched out in a mock embrace, they would have reached the statute's knees. The fingers were wide, more like spatulas than digits, and the breasts were small and full, but the nipples were replaced with small mouths. One featured the tip of a tongue grazing the lips. Lastly, the cunt was a simple, deep hole set in the lower abdomen. But it drew attention thanks to the ring of curved, manicured fingers that hooked inward. He left the face blank, confident that the rest of the body gave off emotion.

The kid touched one of the vaginal fingers gently, as if afraid it might grip his own finger and not let go, dragging his hand inside the piece.

"'Fatal Fem.' Took me two months that one. I can't wait for the women at the gallery to see that one. Those yuppy bitches will probably shit all over their designer panties. Oh, but they'll croon over it. Always do."

Joseph put his hand on Andy's shoulder and he could feel a sudden tenseness, a flinching at the contact. It confirmed his belief that Andy had just begun hustling. Such a raw find outside the bar seemed such a lucky break, and Joseph felt himself grow even more excited about the night.

The boy turned around to face Joseph and he mutely accepted the glass of bourbon of-fered him. As he nervously drank, Joseph slid his hand down the boy's flat chest to the waist, where he gripped at the beltloops of his cutoffs. And just when Andy lowered the glass from his thin lips, Joseph jerked him towards him, until their lips were almost touching.

Andy made a soft cry that seemed more appropriate for a rabbit caught in a trap than a human, and he dropped the tumbler, which shattered on the wood floor. Joseph paid no notice, keeping his eyes locked with the boy's.

"Ever make something, Andy? I mean really sweated over a piece of work for days, weeks, until all that you have inside drains into it. Leaving you a husk, barely able to walk away."

The boy shook his head, his eyes never straying from Joseph's.

"I need something to fill me up again. Something warm and alive. And I can't think of a better medicine than you. How do you taste, Andy? Bitter or sweet?"

He kissed the boy then, crushing his lips against his, thrusting his tongue into Andy's mouth to explore. After a few minutes, Joseph took the boy in tow into the bedroom. His mind raced in anticipation of the bed, of the cruel piece of sharpened brass.

JOSEPH SPENT THE FOLLOWING DAYS IN BED amid sheets soiled with sweat and semen. His mind kept wandering with the aid of the television, the remote control lying as his bed companion. Like an addict recovering from withdrawal, his hands were shaky, lost when not creating with plaster and blood. Senses that had been heightened now suffered downtime.

With the evening news on, Joseph grew drowsy, barely paying attention. The usual junk reports anyway: fires, car crashes, a shooting of a boy. All the same shit. He never understood why so many kids were almost eager to die fast. Joseph preferred his Thanatos urge as muse, and as he drifted back to sleep he wondered what inspiration he would have next.

He awoke to a light sandpaper touch caressing his naked stomach. Joseph opened gummy eyes to see a large rust-colored figure standing over his bed, an arm bent down to deliver a lover's touch.

Startled, he pulled away and sat up, his hand seeking the switch of the bedside lamp. The figure pulled back its arm in response to Joseph's sudden movement.

The yellow light washed over the room, illuminating both Joseph and the figure, revealed to be his latest work.. A long whisper, coated with a sheen of bitter sorrow, came from the featureless face.

"I don't understand... what's happening... why like this... remember goin' back after bad fix... was such a small gun... pain... darkness and now I'm here... like this, why like this? You touched me last... help me... please help me... "

Joseph scrambled to the other side of the bed, nearly falling to the floor in the process. He could feel his head shaking from side to side, knew that his mouth hung open, but only a low moan seemed able to escape from his throat.

The statue began to move around the bed towards Joseph, its stride long and heavy. It reached down and, despite his struggles, picked him up with its malformed hands and brought him screaming to an embrace. Horrified, he watched the small mouths on the breasts begin to open and close, dripping dark red spittle in anticipation of meeting Joseph's flesh.

A soft tickle against the inside of his thigh made him kick and pound the statue even harder. He did not need to look down; in the long days of creation, his mind had envisioned every perverse square inch of the statue. He knew that what he felt were the statue's vaginal fingers undulating, each seeking a firm grip at his naked genitals so that they might guide his cock into the hole they fed.

His own arms were now stretched out before him, one desperately pressing against the statue's shoulder, the other gripping at its face as if seeking to stopper some hidden crack from whence the whispers still seeped from. "Like this... help me... "

But no matter how hard he pushed away, the plaster grip remained tight, slowly pulling him closer. He closed his eyes, not wanting to see anymore.

"I don't fucking want you!" he screamed at his work.

In scraping his fingers raw at the face, he felt the soft edges of the gauze strip. He grasped at it, pulling it away. The strip tore beneath his fingers and he could feel warm liquid cascading down from the neck, over his hands, to splash against his bare chest. In that same horrible whispery voice, the statue screamed and dropped him.

Joseph looked up at the statue from where he lay on the floor and saw how the thing gripped at its neck with a hand, the flat fingers encircling the wound. Fresh blood dripped from its clenched fingers.

He scrambled to the studio, towards the front door. As he passed the kitchen he heard the sound of statue's feet upon the wood floor-boards as it followed after him. He felt a rough hand brush against his back with enough force to break his stride and cause him to trip.

The thing bore down on him again, its whispers now a mere whimper. He reached out as if to ward it off, and his arm struck the metal rod that supported one of the heating lamps. He shoved it between him and the thing, slamming his palm against the floor switch.

The orange light hit the statue, causing it to reel as if struck by something physical. It closed its free hand over one of the large bulbs, and before it crushed the hot metal and glass, Joseph could smell the tang of burning blood.

The thing's wail of pain jarred his spine, and it stepped back from the lamp towards the loft windows behind it.

Seeing hope, Joseph kneeled behind the lamp and pushed it forward towards the creature. The statue retreated to the wall, the open window behind it. Joseph then gave the lamp one last push, praying that it would not topple over before reaching the statue. It stayed balanced, driving the statue farther back, until, with its great weight, it toppled through the window on a blanket of broken wood and plaster and glass. The heating lamp wedged itself across the scarred opening following the thing's four-story plunge.

Joseph ran over, thrusting aside the battered lamp, all the while panting. His throat grew more raw with each gasp he took to catch a proper breath. He had to see, to know that the nightmare over. A pile of broken plaster lay centered in a pool of dark blood on the macadam floor of the alley.

He held his breath and listened. No more whispers.

Relieved, his stomach finally released the tension crushing his insides: Joseph retched right there, bringing up little more than spittle and acid. Wiping his mouth, he made his way to the wall where his tools hung as emblems of his craft. He grabbed the large hammer.

He went into the bedroom and began to strike the headboard's brass piping that he had sharpened so many months ago. His hands were slick from sweat and blood, and often they dropped the hammer, but he would pick it up and start again. He left the headboard unrecognizable, then collapsed on the bed, crying and cursing his artistic vision. While clenching and unclenching the sheets, he ignored the fresh stains he was adding.

Then he stopped and thoughts of the other statues he had made, all for the sake of fame and money and sex, racked his memory. How many were there? Five? Six? Surely more than that. He could not think straight. Instead, images of the quick life of the male prostitute crowded his mind. Drug overdose, a psychotic john, AIDS, an angry pimp? How about even a simple accident. Then they would all come looking for him, their maker, their real sugar daddy. And not all would be pleading with him for help...

He rushed to his office and rumpled through receipts trying to find the addresses of those who had purchased his work. His hands left crimson trails on the blotter and papers he dropped in his haste.

He managed to find a name with matching street address in the city, and he took up the hammer again. Joseph headed towards the door, stopping once he remembered his naked state. He threw on a shirt and pulled on some jeans all while grabbing for his car keys. He struggled with his sneakers, having to finally lean against the wall for balance.

Ready, he opened the door to leave, when he noticed the red palm-shaped stain his hand had left behind on the gray wall. And then he finally realized how much blood he had on his hands.

FINN'S NIGHT

"IT IS YOUR WAGER, I BELIEVE, MR. GARRISON."
Dupre took care in raising the glass to his lips, making sure that all
the men sitting around the card table noticed how awkward the movement was and that he took a healthy gulp. The murky drink of cedar
water only resembled whiskey. Dupre even slouched an inch or so
back in the cushioned seat, to further the illusion of inebriation.

The others had folded. Garrison was sweating and fidgeting like a
little boy in the pew on a hot Sunday. The cattleman surely had more
money on the table than in his wallet, never a wise decision.

His thick hands squeezed the bill before laying it in the center of
the table. "Twenty dollar raise."

"I'll see that, sir." Dupre dropped several gold coins. "Call."

The men on Garrison's side of the table leaned in close as the cattleman turned over his cards to reveal a full house, kings and tens.

"An excellent hand you have, Mr. Garrison." Dupre slowly fanned
out his cards on the table. "'Tis a pity that the ladies, these four queens
and Lady Luck herself, favor me today."

The gambler allowed himself a moment before reaching out to
take his winnings. Garrison sat there, looking pale, his bushy mustache almost drooping at the ends.

"If you pardon me, gentleman," Dupre stood up, lifted his hat and cane from the chair besides him. "It's been a pleasure, but I would like to catch a glimpse of the sunset before the evening repast."

Out on deck, Dupre took out a cigar and idly rolled it in his hand. The sky was darkening, the sun looking almost swollen it was so low and red. He breathed in deeply the air of the Mississippi and, for a moment, let himself be taken back so many years to when he first began plying the riverboat trade, a deck of marked cards in his hand. That was a Dupre who thrilled at every swindle, every winning hand.

Nowadays, his fine clothes fit over a slight paunch, his oiled hair showed a distinguished gray at the edges, his hands were slower with dealing from the bottom of the deck, and that thrill... Dupre sighed. Only the majestic river that he took glory in was the same.

He struck a match against the wooden railing, and the smell of sulfur rushed his face, when he saw one of the lines that led over the side of the boat begin to move. He remained still, watching, forgetful of his customary victory smoke even while the match burned down and singed his fingers. He cursed under his breath and brought his fingertips to his mouth. When he looked back he saw a small hand grab hold of the railing.

Dupre grinned around the cigar and took a few steps backwards, hiding behind the corner wall. A measure of animation began to fill his chest; whomever this interloper was, it promised to make the voyage more exciting.

The boy that pulled himself up over the side of the riverboat and onto the deck was gangly, with skin browned from the sun and cinnamon-colored hair in need of a good combing. His shirt and trousers were ripped and dirty, the uniform of a wharf rat.

But the boy's smile, so wide and showing every ounce of mischief a young boy could possess, was what truly caught Dupre's attention. The young botherment looked about his new environs and grinned at his apparent good fortune.

The boy headed in Dupre's direction, and the gambler slunk back into hiding. As the lad passed by, Dupre held out low the length of his cane, catching the boy between footfalls and sending him with a cry to the boards.

"Terrible thing, these damp decks. Slippery on the feet." Dupre reached down and helped the boy to his feet. He kept a firm grasp on the boy's arm and made a show of looking him over, from top to bottom. "Of course, most of the passengers on this vessel wear shoes."

The boy gave a tentative tug to test Dupre's grip. "Lost 'em when I went overboard. Been tryin' all day to catch up with this boat."

"Overboard? I do not recall any agitation over a lost child."

At the mention of the word 'child,' the boy frowned.

Dupre chuckled and let go of the boy. "Forgive me." He tipped his hat. "Anton Dupre, venturer by trade. And your name is?"

The boy took a step back and considered. "Huck, sir."

"A pleasure." Dupre took the boy's hand in a firm shake. "May I ask the name of the vessel?"

Huck look confused for a moment. "The *Walter Scott*."

"Well, you are standing on a different deck, I'm afraid."

Huck looked about exaggeratedly. "Oh, I meant that I had fallen overboard on a different ship and been out on the river for days 'til this one came near." He turned and started to walk away.

The gambler brought up his cane and laid the tip on the boy's shoulder. "I seem to recall that ship sank over a year ago."

The boy stiffened. He looked over his shoulder at Dupre.

"Seems like you have two choices. You could be foolish and run and know that I will inform the captain of a stowaway."

"Or?"

"If you happen to be a young man looking to see what the night might offer, in terms of adventure —"

Huck nodded.

"Well then, my boy, allow Dupre to be your guide." Dupre actually felt ebullient as he laid a hand on Huck's shoulder and guided the boy towards the dining hall.

The *River's Mercy* was blessed with an exceptional dining hall. Everywhere one looked was the shine of white linen, crystal, and silver, so that the eye ignored everything but the tables. Unless you made your livelihood aboard the vessel and had long since grown jaded to even the most decorous trappings.

The beautiful woman who stood in one of the many doorways, surveying not the finery on the tables but the cut of the suits the men wore, was one such person. When she saw Dupre and the boy entering the hall, she smirked and quickly moved to intercede them before they had reached a place to sit.

"Why, Mr. Dupre, I see you have found yourself a charge." She leaned down and smiled at Huck, running her fingers through his unruly hair. "Or is he a marker?"

Dupre grinned, not altogether pleasantly, at the woman. "My boy, allow me to introduce you to a lady of some renown." He removed his hat and placed it over his heart and gave a slight bow. "Miss Abigail Longley, this is young Huck."

Miss Abigail held out a lavender-colored gloved hand. Huck took her hand without truly knowing what to do. "Nice meetin' ya, Ma'am."

"How precious. Are you joining Mr. Dupre and myself for dinner?" She gracefully tipped her head and hand towards the rest of the hall.

The gambler inwardly groaned at how the woman had once again insinuated herself at his table. Only last month she had sat down next to the local judge Dupre had been courting on the game table all day—that old crow had been ripened for the plucking. The judge did leave the *Mercy* with empty pockets, but only Miss Abigail had the pleasure of sharing his company for the rest of the voyage. In her stateroom, of course.

Still, one had to keep a certain demeanor, no matter what you were dealt. Dupre patted the boy on the shoulder. "Huck, I am sure you are in for a repast that knows no boundaries."

Huck nodded absently as he looked around him.

The three found a table in the farthest corner. Immediately after they sat in their chairs, several dark-skinned waiters, as impeccably dressed as the other furnishings of the ship, unfolded their napkins and laid them in their laps.

Huck shrugged. "Once I stayed with a family that set a table like all this."

"Really?" Dupre expected either a tall tale or the beginnings of a swindle. Either would make dinner all the more interesting.

"Yeah. The Grangerfords." Huck grabbed a roll from the basket and tore into it with his teeth.

"Grangerfords." Miss Abigail dipped just the tip of her finger into a waterglass, then ran it along the edge, making the glass sing. Huck watched, apparently transfixed. "That name sounds familiar."

The boy tried to emulate her but only succeeded in knocking the glass over. Dupre managed to dodge most of the downpour. The servants quickly began the task of cleaning. Huck stayed seated, chewing on the bread.

"Oh yes, didn't they all perish in some terrible feud?"

He nodded. "I spent the last days with 'em." The servants placed a bowl of soup in front of each of them. Huck leaned down and sniffed, scrunching his small nose. "Was friends with their youngest, Buck." He lifted up the bowl and took a tentative sip. The soup was either to his liking or Huck was hungry enough because he began slurping it down as Dupre brought up his spoonful for a taste.

"Huck and Buck. Why, isn't that just charming?" Miss Abigail's laugh could sometimes make Dupre grind his teeth. He dabbed at a drop of the soup that had stayed on his mustache.

"Poor Buck." The boy wiped his chin on his sleeve. He looked down at the empty bowl. "I pulled him from the water and covered his face." He laid the napkin over the bowl in show.

Dupre had long ago become adept at reading faces. And the wistful expression young Huck wore carried enough of a lover's grief that the gambler wondered what had happened between the boys.

Huck stayed in a dismal mood for the rest of dinner, no matter how Miss Abigail tried to ply him with dessert sweets or even more chiming from her glass. Dupre watched and ate, deciding another tack was in order.

"So, my boy, perhaps you would care to help me out in a little game?"

Huck shrugged but did not look away.

"Back home did they ever bother to teach you poker?"

"Course. Usually win too."

Dupre smiled. Ahh, the delightful bluster of youth. At least the challenge had brought the boy's dander up.

"Excellent," Dupre leaned in close, heedless of Miss Abigail's presence. "Well, aboard the Mercy you may be too young to play, but observing the game is another matter. Very simple, really. I want you to sit on a table across from me. If you happen to catch a glance at any of the player's hands—"

"You cheat people?" Huck suddenly asked.

"Oh no, our Mr. Dupre is quite the gentleman. Why I recall one time a banker had lost quite a sum to him at cards." Miss Abigail lifted a dainty hand to her mouth and giggled a moment. "Mr. Dupre arranged to spend some time with the banker's young son—a handsome boy like his father—and the money was returned. Everyone wore a smile at the end of the evening." She giggled again, the sound carrying loudly as the dining room began to empty.

One of the servants removing the dishes scowled. "Best not say such things too loudly, Miss Abigail."

"Indeed," Dupre said between gritted teeth.

"Hush. We all have our indiscretions." She took up her glass of whiskey, as if to make a toast. "Mine is an aversion to any work that doesn't require me to recline," she said with a smile. "And your's, well you do choose a most fresh company to keep." She lightly tapped Huck's head.

Dupre glared at the woman a moment, choosing it best to ignore rather than encourage her. "Huck, cheating is such an awful word." He doubted his argument would have to be thorough; the boy looked far too much the rapscallion. "I simply separate a fool and his money faster than Fate would normally allow. Like a boyhood game, I think."

Huck nodded.

The gambler reached into his vest pocket and pulled out a gold dollar. The boy's eyes widened, and he seemed mesmerized by the glint of the coin as Dupre flipped it up in the air. "Some of your reward for helping me."

Huck reached out and smoothly caught the coin when it flew up the third time.

DUPRE GLANCED UP FROM HIS CARDS. A painted pair. Jacks. Already one of the other players was down to the felt, penniless. As he took in the two men remaining in the game, Dupre watched Huck out of the corner of his eye. The boy sat on an empty table and swung his legs, looking bored. Dupre counted twice the times that his small confederate moved. One of them had two pair. Probably the cattleman from the way his finger kept savoring the edge of his hand.

"Fold." Best to save his money for sweeter cards.

Garrison reacted to his decision with all the grace the Texas range had taught him, a dark and angry look that betrayed his winning hand.

Lady Luck, and the boy, soon delivered most of the money brought to the table to Dupre. But even more thrilling was the sensation that rushed through his veins. An almost forgotten exhilaration, the pleasure of deceit mixed well by cheating

The king of clubs was the only card in front of Dupre that was showing. A good omen, for the local lore had the card named after that infamous Macedonian, who no doubt buggered his way through each conquest. A man after the gambler's own heart. "Alexander here, I believe wants me to raise." He pushed forward a pile of bills, far in excess of what the others could afford to lose on that hand.

He nearly lost his own, the one of flesh. Garrison suddenly slammed his fist down atop the gambler's fingers. Dupre let out a soft cry, more of shock than pain. He looked into his opponent's eyes and saw them wide, almost rolling in their sockets.

"Show yer cards," the cattleman muttered through clenched teeth. His shirt was stained dark beneath his arms and below his neck.

"Calling before you even wager is not how the game is played." Dupre kept his voice calm and did not even try to withdraw his hand, hoping that the man's anger would break apart harmlessly against his cool exterior.

"I think yer a damn cheat. Gots my money this morn, and yer after it now."

When it came down to the crux, Dupre knew that poker truly was not a gentleman's game. All the affectations, the wonderful cloths and glint of gold and jewels, these shows of wealth were merely dupes of the cardsharper to lure the hapless to the table. Invariably, trouble would rear, and Dupre blamed his good mood for not warning him of the danger.

"Perhaps it would be best if I withdrew from the game?"

Garrison lifted up his fist, and for a moment when he saw the man's eyes narrow and Dupre was sure he would have to dodge a blow. Far worse though, was watching him reach under his overcoat and draw out the pistol.

The gun was an ugly thing, dark and oiled, not a cardsmith's derringer but more the sort a highwayman might use.

Dupre glanced at Huck's reaction; at least the boy was wise enough to quietly get down from his table and head towards the door. Watching him slip out of the room in a matter of seconds was both a relief and a regret. He had been growing quite fond of young Huck.

The click of the safety, an ugly sound, brought Dupre's attention back to Garrison.

The others around the table had all leapt to their feet. One man looked nervously back and forth between the gambler and the cattleman. Another began reaching for what little money he had left on his share of the table.

"So," Dupre started, rubbing the bruised fingers of his cigar hand. "I suppose restitution is in order."

Garrison seemed far more nervous behind the trigger than he did a fan of playing cards. "Fancy words, all yer ever sayin' is fancy words." The barrel twitched a little.

Dupre felt a single bead of sweat at his temple underneath his dark slick hair. "Would you like me to return your money?" He paused a moment to let that offer sink in.

Garrison nodded, his scrawny neck bobbing. "Still don't make cheatin right."

Inwardly, subtly, Dupre sighed. The man was crazed with ire. He doubted there would be an opportunity to reach for his own firearm, kept at his ankle. To sit down now might seem too odd of a gesture.

One last attempt at reason and then he would have to risk it. "Pray tell, how have I cheated?"

Garrison started to speak then stopped, his eyes shifting to take in the others. But they were all silent.

The door to the room creaked open. A flurry of pink cotton rushed inside, perilously close to the cattleman who seemed frightened by the sudden intrusion, and wrapped itself around Dupre.

"Papa!"

The gambler looked down to see a little girl pressed against his legs and torso. Strong arms gripped him around the waist. Too strong, he realized. The bonnet covering Huck's head might conceal his lack of long tresses, but Dupre saw that the boy had so hastily dressed in girl's clothing that he had misbuttoned the back and his dirty shirt showed through. The gambler moved his hand to cover the evidence, while trying not to smile as he confronted Garrison.

"Do you intend to fire sir, and make an orphan of my daughter here?"

The cattleman's brow furrowed. His eyes danced over Dupre, the child holding him tightly, even the onlookers. The hand that held the gun shook slightly. Tiny beads of sweat gave his unkempt face an unhealthy sheen.

Dupre glanced down at the card table. "There seems a tidy sum of my winnings here. I believe all of you gentlemen could share the wealth, as it were, including you, Mr. Garrison, and call off any vendettas."

Garrison looked down at the pile of notes and chips. A vein on his forehead began to tremble and Dupre inwardly relaxed and knew that the crisis was over. He took the luxury to rub his 'daughter's' arm. His fingers could feel the taught muscles underneath the flimsy cotton dress.

"I think our Mr. Dupre here's a right generous man," said one of the others. He removed his hat and took a hand to some of the winnings. The rest followed suit, leaving Garrison to realize that unless he acted quickly, he would once more be cheated out of his money. The hand holding the pistol fell to his side, and a moment later he was scavenging like the rest.

Dupre gently pried the boy from him. Huck immediately went around, hiding behind the gambler. Dupre reached for his gilded cane and then doffed his hat. "Gentleman. I think my Rebecca could use a breath of fresh air." He nodded at them all. "It has been most stirring."

Together they walked from the room, only running once the door was shut behind them. Out on deck, it was just the two of them and the river. Both leaned against the railing and grinned at the boy's trickery that they had saved the gambler's hide.

Dupre took a moment to glance at the sky. He was always amazed how nightfall turned the Mississippi into something majestic. The lit moon could be jealous of it's reflection in the dark water, while along the riverbank, the trees gently swayed to an evening breeze that held so many soft sounds and gentle smells, it was impossible to say what was out there.

"Dare I ask where you happened upon these clothes?" He reached out and plucked at the front of the dress.

Huck grinned. "I ran to find a crewmen. But this ship's too big. Ended up by the staterooms. There were this little girl playin' on the carpet. Happened to me before to get out of trouble to dress up like a girl. So I traded the money you gave me to cheat for you."

"I think I very well owe you my life, Huck." He moved closer to the boy, who pulled off the bonnet and ran a hand through his hair. Huck's smile showed a mischievous grin of slightly crooked teeth. "Heh, any chance to play with someone and save a life's worth it."

"Come a step closer," Dupre said even though they were standing so close to one another that there could only be a single step left before they were touching.

Huck did not hesitate. They brushed up against one another. The boy looked up at the gambler.

Dupre leaned down and gently kissed the boy. Huck did not resist, even reached out and held onto the man's shoulder. It may have lasted moments or hours.

"No one's ever kissed me like that."

Dupre smiled, and the expression felt odd on his face until he realized it was a genuine one, not one pulled from his repertoire of smirks. He truly was fond of the boy, could feel a heretofore unknown sense of generosity.

"Tell me, Huck, have you ever slept on a genuine goose-down bed? It truly is like resting on a slice of heaven."

"Been a while, Mister Dupre."

Dupre reached out and ran a few fingers through the boy's hair just above the ear, marveling how soft it felt. "Anton."

Together, with the man resting a hand on the boy's shoulder, and the boy leaning against the man's side, they walked through the closest door towards Dupre's grand stateroom.

RESEMBLANCES

THE OLD STAIRS CREAKED UNDERNEATH HIM. Dave shifted the paper bag of canned goods into his other arm and gripped the long banister. Just one more flight until his floor. He paused, looking at one apartment door and wondering if there was anyone left inside. And if there was, were they the sort to break into another tenant's place and steal something precious?

In his hall, the bulb had broken yet again. He stepped around the circular pattern the shards of glass had made on the industrial carpet. The lock on his door was shiny and new. The key to it was monstrous, all jagged and teethed. He hated both but after last month when he woke up in the middle of the night and found his place a mess, things taken, and the front door wide open, he needed the security.

Inside the studio apartment, he was greeted by static from the radio on the coffee table. He set his package down and tried to find a station. How many were still broadcasting? At last he found a weak voice describing those areas of the city that had Fallen. So far his neighborhood was not listed. But he had his doubts.

His desk was a mess of papers. He pushed aside some ancient sketches and uncovered last month's rent check. No one had knocked on his door for it, and he had not seen another tenant in over two weeks. They must have all departed for safer zones before they cordoned off the area. He picked up the check and tore it in half; the money in his account had already been spent so didn't really matter.

He wanted to have the urge to go into the other side of his studio apartment, to where he kept all his art supplies, and do something with his hands. But he had been dry of inspiration for so long and still felt nothing other than the urge to sleep and listen to the radio spitting dread news. The bed sheets were open, perhaps still a bit warm from this morning. He sighed and went to them.

DAVE WONDERED IF THIS WAS TRULY HIS DREAM. He lay on his stomach on a wide bed. The other boy was there, the one that made his breath catch and his heart ache. The boy lightly dipped a paintbrush into a bucket of dark water. As he lifted the brush over Dave, a few drops fell upon his bare arm. Each was bitterly cold, and if the other was not holding him down he would have twisted out of the way. The rough bristles lightly touched the skin around his shoulder blade. A tap. Then another wet, chilled tap.

"I remember you once mentioned in front of the mirror how you'd like a tattoo here." The other boy breathed out deeply, perhaps a sigh. "I loved the idea. Let me help."

Dave woke suddenly, his heart pounding. Always these days he would find dreams of him. Maddening, alluring, just too damn much for any artist. Was this all he could do? Dream of someone warm and close, like a forbidden brother, yet when awake stare at blank paper and canvas?

He rose up and went to the bathroom. In the mirror the face that had been called adorable or beautiful on occasion seemed totally unwholesome. The eyes seemed sunken, the jaw haggard. Was he truly only twenty-two? Had lack of sleep the past week aged him, or was it all because he had stopped caring about anything anymore, now that he could not work?

He closed his eyes a bit, blurring the reflection. It now reminded him of someone else. But he chased away thoughts of his dream and of the arms of the other boy. He needed to be awake, at least for another day.

So he turned the taps, heard the water groan out and hit the old porcelain. He splashed his face again and again, turning fierce, so that it was more like a wet slap against his shoulders and neck. Finally he exhausted himself and groped and turned off the taps.

He could not tell if what dripped down off his face into the sink was the water or tears.

THE LAST THING HE HAD DRAWN WAS GONE. With it some clothes and cash, but that had been enough to break his spirit. He had spent days on the drawing, sometimes moving the pencil so finely his eyes ached following his hand. What had started as a self-portrait had evolved into something different. Shorter hair, no scar marring the forehead from that car accident. Thinner lips, more apt to smile. Someone he would want to see. Maybe even hold and kiss.

It had won last year—the Haddon Township Art Show—only a blue ribbon, but that had been enough to keep him elated for days. He had not wanted to draw again for a while, just simply ride the high and see where it would lead him.

And then came the Fall and an obsession to see where that would lead to also. Dread and worry kept him from his charcoals and pencils and paint. Pinned to the upper edge of his desk were newspaper clippings about the Fall. The one he stared the most at was dated two months ago. A photograph of a city block, perhaps only a mile from here. Reality had fled and left a building's facade peeling away like a rind, revealing the skeleton of fossil wood. What would the Fall bring to this building? What would happen to him? Such thoughts left him panicked, sometimes barely able to breath.

HE WAS SITTING IN ONE OF THOSE OLD-FASHIONED loveseats, thickly upholstered with delicate lace on the armrests. He wasn't alone. He never was when he dreamt anymore. The other boy was there, his presence a comfort though they were not holding hands. Yet. In front of them hung a mirror, suspended in mid-air, and unframed, a razor sheet of glass. One reflection, but Dave was not sure which one of them it was.

The other boy turned to him, bent closer and started to whisper and lick Dave's ear. He couldn't catch the words, but they were something wonderful, he was sure.

"Oh, wake up."

Sitting on the window ledge was a young man. Black jeans and ash-gray t-shirt made his skin stark white by comparison. His dyed-black hair was thick and wavy and unruly. He lifted and stretched out a leg, making his seat precarious what with the open window and three-story fall. No shoes or socks, just pale feet. The face was interesting enough to notice twice.

"Who the fuck are you?" The words came out slow and weak. Dave blinked away the last remnants of his dream.

"Nice mouth. I'm Caleb." He said it like his name was almost obvious. Or infamous.

Dave wiped a hand across his face and muttered. This was insane.

The boy chuckled as he slipped down from the window ledge. He headed towards the open closet door. "Interesting floor you picked to live on. Down the hall there's an apartment that they rent out every three weeks because the tenants disappear regularly. Your next-door neighbor has something nasty growing under his bed. And you had Haddon."

"What the hell are you talking about?" Dave sat up in bed. How had this nut managed the treacherous climb up four stories to come through an open window?

"Relax. I just want to have a little talk." There was a slight edge to the words. "And grab the photograph."

The stranger casually walked around, stopping at the closet where he leaned against the door. Dave crawled out of the bed. He wore only the boxers from yesterday. He saw how Caleb looked him over appreciatively. It made him reach for the jeans and sweatshirt on the floor.

"Like father, like son."

"I don't understand anything you're saying." A thought suddenly occurred to him. That this Caleb must have been the one that robbed him before and must be so desperate that he returned again. Anger began to flare up, coupled with unease. He couldn't help but be nasty. "So, what are you going to swipe this time?"

One blackened eyebrow rose. "Fine words from someone trying to steal my boyfriend."

Dave shut his mouth. That was certainly not the response he had expected. Boyfriend? It had been months since he had been out socially. Perhaps longer since he had last dated, hell even slept with another boy. This Caleb must have been walking through a Fallen Area and had his brains spindled.

"Don't look so innocent. I came here and caught you with him. In bed." He pointed towards the tangled sheets.

"My dreams?"

Caleb nodded. He took a few steps closer to where Dave stood. "At least Haddon has good taste."

"This is all impossible..."

"Please. You're living in a Fallen Area. What did you expect to happen?" He paused for a moment but Dave just stood there feeling lost. "You just can't know. No one ever knows what might happen."

His anger returned anew. "Who the fuck is Haddon?"

Caleb sighed. He turned around and the closet door swung open of its own accord. Inside was a mixture of hanging clothes, wrapped packages and taped boxes.

"He was in there."

Dave watched as Caleb grabbed the nearest thing. The brown paper unfolded at his touch, leaving naked a white board filled with charcoal musings. "Not bad, but he was your best piece. He likes to wear blue, 'cause of the ribbon he earned."

Understanding was a harsh blow to Dave. He even clutched his stomach as if punched, stepping back and back until his calves struck the bed. What this boy was talking about—or was that who he talked about—could only be Dave's last drawing. But pen and ink made flesh was insane. Unless of course he truly did live where everything had gone wrong.

Caleb smirked at Dave's reaction. He held up a shoebox. The lid slipped off without being handled. All the little slips of memories fell onto the floor in a rain of papers.

"Where's the photograph?"

Dave stared at the pile on the floor. Glimpses of cars and spheres and other assignments from art school waited to be scooped up and protected from a stranger's eyes. He barely heard Caleb.

"What?"

"Your picture. The one you used to make Haddon."

Dave tried not to think of himself as anyone's creator, especially not some twin. "Why do you want it?"

Caleb shrugged. "Maybe it will sever the link you share." He ran a hand through his hair, looking for a moment tired. "You never know how jealous you can be until you wake up next to your lover and see that he's still sleeping and he's harder for his dreams than he ever was for you."

"Maybe you're not the one for him." Dave said it softly, more to himself than to Caleb. A part of him was slowly accepting all this, buying into the madness.

"Nice fucking incestuous image you're thinking." Caleb turned around and kneeled down to the floor and began touching everything in the closet. Wrappings pulled loose, clothes unbuttoned, boxes flew open and sprayed out their contents.

Dave grimaced at what was being done, but he didn't trust that he could stop Caleb from hunting. "Guess Haddon didn't pick you for your attitude." Still, he caught himself looking at the boy's ass wondering if it was smooth and pale like the parts he could see.

"Damnit!" Caleb turned over until he was lying on the floor, his upper body still within the confines of the closet. He shut his eyes tight. "It's not in here, is it?"

"No."

"You like your dreams with him." He almost stuttered the sentence out.

"I guess." Dave rubbed his face. The memories of the dreamt moments shared with Haddon stirred him. "It's all strange. Everything he does moves me. So yeah, I do."

"Fuck." Caleb stamped the hardwood floor with both feet. "I've waited too long to find someone like him." He pushed himself to a sitting position and looked up at Dave. He held out a hand. "Help me up."

Dave considered for a moment, and then offered his hand. When Caleb grasped it, he pulled and felt how light the boy was. He must be only skin and bones under that T-shirt.

They were inches apart and Caleb was staring deeply at him. Dave averted his eyes unexpectedly.

"You're a handsome son-of-a-bitch. I can see some of Haddon in you." He slowly lifted up a hand and went to touch Dave's cheek.

Dave turned his head and felt the hand fall upon the back of his head. Caleb's fingers lightly played in his long hair. "Wrong. It's the other way around. Some of me is in Haddon."

Caleb shrugged. "Perhaps." He stepped back and glanced about the room. "The photograph. Open up to me."

Something took hold of Dave's throat. Nothing painful but he found himself forced to speak, as if coaxed by some weird pressure. Words came out rough and raw, not in a voice he liked. "The dresser."

"Much better." Caleb turned back. He wore an embarrassed expression.

All the dresser doors slid open as he approached. The top one was filled with motley things, memories attached to each one. Caleb slipped his hand inside and pulled out the photo. A black and white shot of Dave, taken two years ago. The face had lines of ink, altering it, but there was still enough there to see the resemblance.

Caleb spent a few moments looking it over. He glanced back at Dave and tapped the edge of the picture to his chin. "I prefer you with the shorter hair." He then took the photo in both hands and tore it in half.

Dave felt like his own insides were torn. Was that it? Were all those wondrous dreams, the ones that had once been frightening but now he wanted, were they all gone?

"I suppose you think me quite the bastard now?" Caleb tore each half apart until there was nothing left but checkered droppings that he let fall to the floor.

Dave nodded absently, staring at the photograph's remains. He could not express to himself how he felt, let alone would he spare any words for Caleb.

"I don't always play well with others." Caleb headed for the bathroom door. "Some advice." The boy bit his lip a moment. "No, I suppose I'm simply telling you. All this," he raised his arms and motioned about him, "is nothing compared to the rest of the Fallen city. You wouldn't last a day there. So don't give any thought to finding out if an awake Haddon is any better."

The bathroom door opened for Caleb who had not taken a step. Beyond was different. Not the room with its cracked tiles and rusted drains. But someplace else, what looked like the street corner down below. Dave turned away; he felt awful enough. To watch Caleb walking away the victor, would be too much to bear. He heard the door close gently.

H E   W O K E   T O   T H E   R A D I O ' S   S T A T I C .   N O   M O R E local broadcast. Everything must have been swallowed up. His dreams had been like the static: annoying and empty. He thought about Haddon, somehow flesh. How much the twin were they? Or had Haddon changed, slowly developing his own unique identity? Absently, he grew hard imagining the boy of his dreams naked in bed, perhaps his own bed. The mental image widened to let in Caleb; he welcomed the picture, guided it as dark clothes were thrown aside to make for naked twistings and tumblings. He was distractingly hard now.

Dave did not stay in bed long. Instead he went to the corner of the studio where he kept his materials. He soon found the roll of pristine white paper and began to sketch with a fever he had never felt before. His hand demanded total control at a maddening pace. Still, some details were already fading. Had the eyes been so dark? The nose so sharp?

Not that it truly mattered. The drawing didn't have to be perfect. Just as he had once done with his own photo, only a resemblance of Caleb was necessary. When he stopped because his fingers ached, there was still much to be done. He sat back and wondered where his suitcase might be. He'd pack tonight, then finish the drawing deeper inside the Fallen. What he would end up with he wasn't sure, but that was all right. Caleb could use some competition after all.

TEA TIME WITH CORN DOLLY

SHE SAT ON THE WINDOWSILL SIPPING TEA, anxious to wet her insides. A breeze passed by and she rustled, which always made Corn Dolly blush and worry that someone close by would hear. But no one seemed to notice. Everyone was busy chatting and laughing or whispering over their cups and mugs of hot tea. The entire shop smelled of steam and spice.

She adjusted her skirt absently. The street outside was nearly empty and in another hour or so, when night fell, it would look forlorn. She wouldn't stay out too late, even if she wanted to. The Bakelite purse by her foot on the sill only had five dollars to spend. She wasn't going to trade any of the AA batteries or the tin of chewing tobacco that she had found for anything less than a meal and tea.

"How's the wistful girl doing?"

The voice startled her. Caleb leaned up against the wall inches away. As usual he was dressed somberly. A pity because she hated the color black. She wondered if he dyed his hair.

"Just okay." She slightly shrugged.

He almost grinned. "Why does it seem you always look ready to sigh?"

"Because I cannot cry." Her standard line. It seemed trite even to her, but habit made her say it.

"Not the Afflicted bit." He took a drink from a slender metal flask. Definitely not tea.

She tried to look sternly at him, but doubted it worked. "People are scared away—"

"Not everyone. You need only find one. One boy who will be gentle." He motioned to the crowd inside the tea shop. "Half of them are so wrong, it's sickening. Inside for the wrong reason, with the wrong person," he raised the flask in a mock toast in her honor, "drinking for so many wrong reasons."

"Still despondent over Haddon?"

His answer was a just a bitter smile with a slight nod of the head.

Poor Caleb. Pining even after a year. Who ever said it was better to lose love than never have it? Losing seemed far crueler. "What's a drunk Opener like?"

He shook his head. "Not very pretty. Especially when I think it's rubbing alcohol."

She laughed. Then her gaze fell on the boy. She didn't normally stare, but the manner he made his way through the crowd of people in the tea shop made her. Other people were looking him over also. His fresh clothes and full backpack blurted out 'newbie.' Even his face, with a small nose and perfect cheekbones, looked newly scrubbed. Corn Dolly watched as he stood in front of the chalkboard menu, idly tapping a dainty porcelain teacup as he read.

"Ahh, see. Never ceases to amaze me what comes in through the door." Caleb chuckled. "Stake your claim now on the morsel before someone else does."

She turned to admonish him but he was already gone.

The boy must have sensed everyone staring and started to glance around and fidget. He finally noticed her by the open window. She gave him a slight smile before looking down at her own cup, then quickly raising her eyes to see him returning the smile. She blushed; boys found her silky blond hair and soft features pretty she knew, but she didn't usually dare be flirtatious. One wrong touch at her wrist or her neck and she'd be crushed.

The boy grabbed a mug in his other hand from the drying stack on a nearby card table. She was surprised when he came over to her.

"I could never sit up there. I'm afraid of heights." He gave a small grin that made Corn Dolly want to wiggle her toes, but the seeds inside would rattle, so she resisted.

"It's not that high." She glanced out the window. The street below was maybe six feet. Even if it was twenty or even a hundred she wouldn't have been hurt by the fall. She always landed light.

"I'm Jamie, and—"

"And you're new around here."

He chuckled. "And I was about to ask what tea you think I should get. But, yeah," he said with a nod. "I am the new boy." She noticed his eyes were a dazzling green.

"Oh. Sorry. Friends call me Dolly." She carefully slipped down from her perch. She took her purse and cup with her. "They have the best tea here."

"What were you drinking?" He lifted the mug in his right hand, showing off faded 'Drink Me' printed besides an upwards arrow.

"Harvest tea. You having two cups?"

Jamie laughed. "No, this is for the little kid outside."

"Oh, you met T."

He nodded. "Yeah, he was just sitting on the steps singing 'tea time' over and over while holding an empty cup. So I asked if he wanted some tea and you should have seen how his face lit up."

"Awww," murmured Corn Dolly. She always liked T. She didn't have the heart to tell Jamie that T wasn't a boy. Or a little girl for that matter. Not easy to explain, and she wasn't too sure she really understand what T really was. That's how being Afflicted works, you're just hard to explain.

"Well I think he'll like the Winter's Tithe. It's sweet."

They stood together in line. While waiting she asked the obvious question, the one the boy probably had grown tired of: why had he come Inside?

He nodded as if expecting her to ask. "'Bout a year ago this girl I was seeing and I were in some trouble. Stupid shit." He shook his head a few times. "We talked about running away, and the Fallen Area always kept coming up. I mean, we heard all sorts of things. Seems like some days that's all anyone ever talks about is what life would be like Inside.

So we did something really dumb. Robbed a liquor store. Fake gun, so don't worry, I'm not dangerous or anything. But the clerk had a real one, pointed it right at me," Jamie lifted up the mug and tapped it to his forehead. "I was scared, paralyzed even, and Sarah, the girl, she took off and left me there. Ended up with ten months in Juvenile Hall."

"And then you wanted In?"

He nodded. "Yeah, well, after the first week I got a letter from Sarah. She was sorry what happened and wrote that she was heading for the Fallen and I should look her up when I got here."

Corn Dolly laughed, the sound light, and she felt bad when she did, but the boy was so new he was clueless. "You think you're going to find her?"

He shrugged. "Maybe. Not sure I even want to anymore."

At that she inwardly sighed in relief. They reached the front of the line. A woman worked the huge vats and tureens, her apron holding shiny ladles and spoons.

"Winter's Tithe, please."

The woman picked up what looked like old leaves covered in snow in a basket. The snow fell off sounding like sand. She dropped them into the nearest pot and stirred for a few moments. Then she filled the two mugs with something brown. Corn Dolly followed back to the front door.

On the bottom step sat a little boy, or maybe a girl, it was hard to be sure with the harshly cut brown hair and wide eyes and small nose. But Corn Dolly knew that T was at best both or maybe neither. She would never dare ask and T never gave any clue. He/she wore a dirty knit sweater and poorly mended jeans. His/her knees were drawn up to the chest. "Tea time, tea time," chimed the little one.

Jamie sat down on one side of T, setting his own mug between his feet and handing over the cup. Corn Dolly sat on the step at T's other side.

The kid stopped singing and actually made a cooing sound at the sight of the full cup in his or her hands. He/she took a tentative sip, then gave both of them a broad smile. Jamie took a sip from his own mug.

Corn Dolly watched them both, feeling oddly content. She wondered if Jamie would be so relaxed and happy if he knew that both T and herself were Afflicted. She wished he would be.

"Tasseomancy's fun." T had drained the cup and smacked his/her lips.

"What was that?"

Corn Dolly ran her hand through T's hair. "Reading tea leaves." She could tell by Jamie's odd look that he was thinking of gypsies and fortune telling, like they were in some old black and white movie.

Jamie drained the rest of his tea. At the bottom of the mug were some dregs, lumps of wet leaves and gray sugar that hadn't dissolved. He tipped the mug in the direction of T. "So what does this mean, then?"

The kid leaned over. Corn Dolly was always envious how thick his/her eyelashes were. Models would kill to have eyes like that. "Hmmm," the kid muttered. "Love." Then T dipped his/her pinkie into the mug. It came out smeared dark at the tip. He/she stuck it in his mouth and smacked his/her lips at the taste. "Bittersweet." T giggled a moment. "Maybe you love tea as much as I do."

A shadow spread over Jamie's face before Corn Dolly could see his reaction to what T said. She looked up to see a girl come near until she was so close as to be practically on top of Jamie. Corn Dolly felt instantly uneasy; not that the girl's purple-dyed hair, shaved to the scalp except for a few long locks in the front, looked awful. No, Corn Dolly remembered seeing the girl lurking about not far from the front gate to the Fallen. She was a member of the Glyphs, a bad bunch Inside. They once threw rocks at Corn Dolly and one stone had punched a hole in her stomach. She had to walk to the infirmary at the shelter to get it stitched up. The wound took weeks to close over.

Things turned worse when Jamie's reaction was not the scowl she hoped for. He rose from the step. They stared at each other for several moments, and then each of their faces softened.

"Jamie!" Her happy shout almost frightened T, who had drawn closer to Corn Dolly. The Glyph threw her arms around Jamie. She kissed him then, short and quick, her tongue barely slipping past his lips. "You made it." She stepped back and looked him over a second time. "You actually made it."

"Yeah." He was almost laughing.

Corn Dolly looked away, feeling emptier than ever. Why had she even bothered being hopeful? Out of the corner of her eye she saw T tug at Jamie's arm. "More please."

Jamie looked down at T, then looked at Corn Dolly. She dared to stare back into his eyes. They were intensely green, almost captivating.

"Stay for one last cup." Her voice sounded unsteady to her, an unspoken begging 'please,' but he smiled and nodded before turning back to the Glyph.

"Sarah, come on in with us. Won't take more than a sec."

Sarah's eyes glared at Corn Dolly and T but the rest of her slouched into a pout. "There's this bash not far from here. Let's go now. It'll be fun," she ran a black-painted fingernail along the crease of his neck. "Like old times."

He took a step away from Sarah and took the offered cup from T. He went quickly up the first few steps to the tea shop. "Right after this, okay?"

The Glyph groaned and for a moment Corn Dolly was sure she'd refuse. But then Sarah followed, practically stomping on each step with her worn, steel-tipped boots. When the Glyph reached Jamie, she threw an arm around his waist. Corn Dolly hesitated, unsure if she should even bother. After all, her heart was as fragile as the rest of her. But the memory of the boy's smile was too strong to abandon.

Enough of the patrons recognized Sarah as a Glyph to cause an uneasy silence throughout the tea shop. Jamie must have become conscious of the disquiet and the stares; he started to look around cautiously.

The sudden smell of harsh liquor stung Corn Dolly's nose. Caleb walked up right beside her, his step more than a little unsteady. "Oh, look at this. A little scribble and her boy."

Sarah turned around and, seeing Caleb, flaunted her middle finger. "Oh look, the freak has a Talented friend."

Corn Dolly was shocked by the girl's bluster. Either she had just earned her first tattoo—the marks that set the Glyphs apart from everyone else in the Fallen—or she was an utter idiot. Caleb had a reputation worse than the Glyphs. Seemed you either owed him, feared him, or worried over how far his friendship would take you.

She knew something awful was about to happen. Everyone did. The whole tea shop had become still. Cups and mugs were poised in mid-sip, the whole room held its breath waiting. All of them made Corn Dolly feel overwrought and wanting to flee.

Even if Caleb didn't start the fight, he'd end it, making a mess of Sarah, maybe opening up her mouth so wide her jaw cracked. Corn Dolly heard he did that once. And then Jamie would probably look at both of them in horror and he'd hate her. Or worse, fear her.

Anything but that.

So she stepped in front of her friend, blocking his view of the Glyph. She put her hands on Caleb's face, feeling how cool his skin was even after the drink had brought an ever-so-slight flush to his ivory cheeks. "Please, Caleb, don't do this," she whispered.

The line of sight broken, his eyes turned on her. She saw a moment's flare of drunken anger and then they cleared. She felt him gently take hold of her, arms wrapping around her.

"Let me. It will make me feel sooo much better." His grin was awful and his breath reeked of whatever he had been drinking. It might really have been rubbing alcohol.

Behind them sounded the giggle of the Glyph. She was baiting them. Corn Dolly could feel Caleb tense all over. She pressed her forehead against his. This was almost too hard to ask, to really say.

"Don't. For me. I'll never ask another favor."

He moved his head to glance around her, his eyes narrowing at whatever they saw. He practically growled out, "But you like this boy. I know it. Let me take her out and—"

Corn Dolly shook her head slowly no and fought back tears. For a moment he just stared at her, and she worried that this was somehow more than he could do, that she had stepped too far. Then she felt first against her body his sigh and the release of his hate.

"Only for you."

Corn Dolly turned around, leaning back against Caleb for support. Jamie stood there looking all the more confused. Sarah's stance was part of the challenge; she looked ready to fight. Or maybe flee. Her eyes moved fast between them, hinting at nervousness.

"Just go." Corn Dolly had to say it twice. The first time the words broke apart in a hastily caught sob.

The Glyph grinned, looking ugly, just so ugly to her. She grabbed hold of Jamie's wrist and started to pull him out of the shop. He actually turned back a moment to look at her. Corn Dolly averted her eyes. Far better, she told herself, not to watch him go.

Minutes after they went out the door, the tension broke in the shop, though the talk that returned was low and sporadic. Caleb glared at the entrance.

"This is fucked up. You like that boy." He took a step away from her and nearly stumbled. She reached out to hold him, trying to grip him as hard as she could. "I'm going after them and bring him back."

Corn Dolly wanted to tell him 'yes' and 'please,' but was about to suffer with another admonition when he tore loose of her hold. Like autumn leaves, the fingers of her right hand drifted down to the floor.

Dropping to her knees, she clutched her ruined hand to her chest, barely feeling the whisper of her heartbeat above the pain. The patrons drew close, but she ignored all their mutters and offers of help. Finally, the light tread of footsteps came near. "Jamie," she whispered.

She looked up to see T there, his/her small hand holding out a cup of tea. "Bittersweet."

Corn Dolly shook her head politely no, desperately wanting to cry. But the tears, as always, never came.

THE ANTHVOKE

Dearest Clay,

You're going to be sad reading this, I know. Jess and I took off for the Fallen Area. I can hear that groan— or are you cursing? But I had to. Ever since she heard of the Fallen, Jess has been obsessing about running away and becoming part of the strangeness. There were nights she never slept, just lay next to me, and I knew she was wondering what was beyond the concrete walls and barbed wire quarantining parts of the city.

I told her she's special and different from everyone else, but that didn't seem to satisfy her. I think she needs to prove it.

Thanks for letting us stay the last few days with you. I hope everything works out with you and that film student.

So indebted to you it hurts,

Marie

THE TWO HAD SPENT THE PAST FEW HOURS ON the streets of the Fallen Area. Along the way their hands often met, not just to help each other along but for that reassuring interweaving of fingers. Overhead, clouds streaked across an angry red sky. Marie, winded from their fast pace, looked up at Jess for strength. Her lover's dark curls had become matted with sweat, but those almost-black eyes shimmered with expectation. Marie had considered stopping to catch her breath many times but always pressed on. But now, so close to their goal, she needed to rest. Her legs and sides burned. She stopped, heaving in gulps of air.

Jess seemed surprised that they weren't moving anymore. She looked over at Marie. "I'm glad you're here with me." That was Jess's way of saying "I love you," to use different words that were easier to admit.

Marie was slightly bent over, hands on her knees, but she still nodded. "This isn't the kind of place I want us to be."

Jess glanced down the street they found themselves on. To Marie, it looked abandoned, with shattered storefronts and debris piled alongside the pavement.

"Can't you find someone else to learn from?" Marie said.

Jess made that face, the one that mixed scolding and pleading. "Hon, we've talked about this before. Anyone other than an anthvoke would want something from me in return. Anthvokes aren't interested in flesh." She tugged at the front of her sweat-stained tank top, briefly revealing the butterfly tattoo over her petite breasts. "Do you really want to share me with someone else?" Her hand reached out and caressed Marie's smooth round face.

Marie answered by taking Jess's hand in her own. Together they cautiously explored what once had been Antiques Row. "Which one is it?"

Jess was silent. She seemed focused on each entrance, the ones that were nothing more than gaping holes framed with jagged glass, the ones boarded up and marred with graffiti, the ones that were choked by boxes filled with trash.

She finally stopped a few feet in front of one shop. The remains of a rolltop desk, thick-limbed mahogany chairs, and a battered samovar that had turned a sick green from the elements were all partly protected by a twisted and rusted grate. The gate's smaller brother blocked most of the open doorway.

"Guests." The voice barely escaped from the darkness inside the shop.

Jess slipped a sweaty hand from Marie's grasp and moved closer, pulling at the metal grate to widen the gap. One of the sharp ends caught and tore the fabric of her batik dress. Marie inwardly shuddered and worried about tetanus. "I've come to learn," Jess shouted. "You have to teach me!"

Marie found herself clutching the brick wall of the shop. This was not her place; she did not feel a guest, not even welcome here. She nearly leapt and climbed the wall when the front of the desk suddenly rolled back on its own. "Students," came the voice, stronger and deeper than before, "are the best guests." The sound of glass being crunched underfoot followed the words. An unkempt man appeared in the storefront window. Greasy hair hung down into his face. He wore the faded scraps of an old smoking jacket. Fresh blood from the debris he was walking through covered his scarred feet. Without a word, or an expression on his unshaven face, he sat down on the only upright chair and stared at the women there on the sidewalk.

Jess reached out towards the man, one of her fingers reverently touching the tattered hem of the jacket. The sight turned Marie's stomach. She wanted to drag Jess back and run that hand under hot water to wash away the traces of the man and this dump. Then they could slip under clean covers and fall asleep safe together.

But she remained still. Jess wanted this.

Clay,

> *You'll never see this letter, but I need to write you anyway. I have no one else to talk to, and I need to talk so badly. I hope you never see where we're living. I'll call it an apartment but it's actually the third floor of an office building. It's close enough to the anthvoke for Jess to walk but gives me the distance I need to feel comfortable. I leave the lights on all the time because row after row of empty cubicles/empty desks in the*

dark would give me nightmares.

That's a lie. I still have nightmares. I wake up on a sleeping bag on the industrial-strength carpet and I'm scared to close my eyes again.

Everything we heard about the Fallen Area on the Outside was pretty much true. But we never heard about the atmosphere. Everything is either abandoned or run down and yet there are people living here! Some streets aren't safe to walk down.

I always feel on edge, worried. As for Jess, well, ever hear of an anthvoke? Prob not. They're Talented with a capital T which just means they can do weird things. Anthvokes somehow tap and awaken the spirit of antiques and old junk. At least, that's how Jess explains it. Nothing make sense. I think the world has gone a little crazy around here. Or am I the only one, since I doubt everything? No, that's not true. I don't have doubts. I hate everything here.

Ugh, that anthvoke. Jess doesn't know how much he bothers me. They wouldn't let me stay and watch her first night of training cause I'm normal, so I waited half the night on an empty street. Nothing to do but try and stay awake. You do not want to fall asleep outside here.

I'm hoping she comes home soon. I'm tired of photo-copying my hand. I've taped pages of me flipping the finger on every door as a warning for others to stay out.

Are film students any easier than Jess?

Missing you,

Marie

"THEY HAVE PAWNSHOPS HERE?" MARIE adjusted the nylon fanny pack around her waist. It lay like a swollen lump against her stomach, stuffed with pepper spray, the cellophane-wrapped caramels that Jess loved, tissues, a Swiss army knife, and, hidden away in the secret zipper compartment, some cash. She felt more confident wearing the pack, as if it were a comic book heroine's trusted utility belt, proof against all the dangers around them. Jess said it made her look fat.

"Uh-huh," Jess nodded absently, as they walked down the stairs to the office building's lobby.

"So is this like homework?"

Jess looked over her shoulder at Marie as she pushed open the glass door to the street and laughed. That laugh, once so common that Marie heard it every day, seemed a stranger's. "I guess you could say that. He told me I need some old things in the apartment to create the right emanations."

Marie bit back her remarks about their "apartment." Bad-mouthing the office had become a habit over the past two weeks—hough by now she almost slept through the nights, and her days spent roaming the vast floor, peering into desk drawers for forgotten bits of clerical treasure, were almost calming. Last night she'd awarded an hours-late Jess with a necklace of rainbow-colored paper clips.

Why the anthvoke just didn't lend Jess junk from his shop was beyond Marie.

The warm weather drew others to the street. Marie envied Jess's ability to simply walk along staring straight ahead, undistracted. Marie could not stop herself from staring at every person passing by. She had the urge to judge, to brand each of them. Those over there seemed normal. Were they stressed and forlorn like herself? She needed a beer. Did desperate people crave beer? She wiped away the dampness of sweat from her upper lip. She struggled to keep her gaze someplace safe, on Jess's back, admiring Jess's wing-like shoulder blade as it moved beneath her pale skin. If she worried about the others around them, she risked breaking down, becoming a wreck.

The pawnshop was thankfully not that far. Past the door was a room with a counter and then a long area behind that filled with boxes and crates that she doubted held anything more interesting than warped record albums and old men's magazines. Marie glanced at the faded pictures of cheap and greasy Chinese food dishes above the counter and her stomach gurgled. What a pity, she thought, to give up shredded chicken with garlic sauce for a shop worse than a second-rate flea market.

The proprietor wore a short-sleeve dress shirt stained along the collar and under the arms from sweat. He looked up from tinkering with an old rotary phone. His glasses enlarged his beady eyes.

"It's not ready yet." He tapped the metal dial of the telephone with the screwdriver he held.

Jess shook her head. "That's not what I need. Or is it?" She tilted her head in thought, and then frowned. "No, not now." She pointed over the proprietor's shoulder on the right. "There, on the third shelf from the top."

The man nervously looked behind him, and then nodded several times, his head bobbing on a thin neck. He stretched out his arms and took down a slightly tarnished silver dome resting on a rosewood base. He carefully placed it on the counter in front of Jess.

"What is it?" Marie took a step closer, actually curious.

Jess took the knob at the top of the dome in her fingers and lifted, revealing a thick layer of metal honeycombed with small round holes. "A vintage cigarette holder. 1943. Made in Trenton, New Jersey."

"How did you know all that?"

"Let me guess," said the store owner, pushing up his glasses over his nose for a moment before they drooped back down again. "You're an anthvoke."

"Nearly," Jess said with a half-smile.

"Ugh, don't start smoking." Marie detested the scent of cigarette smoke.

"I'll take it." Jess lowered the dome back into place. "How much is it, anyway?"

"Trade or cash?"

"Cash." Marie unzipped the fanny pack and took out the money.

He thought for a moment, biting at his lip and looking disappointed that there would be no trade. "Then it's thirty."

"What about that tea cup?"

Twenty minutes later, they left the store with two bags full of treasure. Jess grinned. Marie allowed her lover's happiness to infect her a little.

"I'm surprised you didn't buy that music box."

"It was a reproduction. Made in Taiwan last year."

"Oh."

Clay,

Well, we've nearly run out of money. Jess doesn't seem worried, even at the thought of no food in the little fridge. Of course, she barely eats anyway. I'm always stuffing my face. Ugh, I think I've gained twenty pounds since we came here. What else am I supposed to do? There's nothing here for me, nothing but Jess, and I'm not so sure she even cares I'm around. We've stopped, well, being intimate. She comes home near morning, wakes me up, and lets me put my arm around her and then she's asleep and I'm left hoping.

Jess promises that as soon as she's mastered her talents, everything will be different and we'll be wanting for nothing. Doesn't she even see that's a lie? I mean, her teacher is this hermit huddled away from the rest of the world with his relics. She brings home all this old crap, staring at it, touching it. Ugh. I try to talk with her, tell her I'm worried, sometimes even scared. But I can tell she's not really listening. She's slowly closing me off.

I miss television. And cheesecake, especially covered with choc sauce. And walking by the river just before dark. I miss you and even those annoying yapping lap dogs of yours. How does your film student stand them?

But neither of us can go back.

Marie

ONE OF MARIE'S MOST RELAXING PASTIMES had always been watching Jess dress. On the Outside, Marie would have been lying on her stomach on their bed while her lover riffled through the closet they shared. Now, in their office apartment, she had to make do with reclining on a sleeping bag and staring up as Jess lifted clothes from a desktop. Her lover chose something she'd bought the other day at a thrift store. Jess let out a giggle as she pulled the old outfit over her head and down her torso. Marie doubted the frayed straps would hold.

"See how it shimmers when I move."

Marie stayed quiet. The fabric had lost most of its gold sequins; the dress had barely survived the ages since a flapper had last worn it. If there was any shimmer left, it was only a last-ditch attempt at glamour. But it did no good to say anything. All the clothes that Jess had brought with her to the Fallen Area were now in the alleyway beside the building, thrown one by one out the window as she brought home vintage things to wear. Marie had managed to hold her tongue when that soft mocha-colored dress she had bought Jess in New Hope on their last anniversary had been consigned to the rats below.

Clay,

Okay, I finally found something here for me. After so many days staying inside, boredom was driving me crazy, so I started exploring the neighborhood. A few blocks away there's a shelter. They offer beds and whatever food people have scavenged. The people that run it were thrilled when I mentioned I was a nurse and wanted me to run a first aid station in the back corner. Yesterday I started helping out.

It felt soooo good.

You'd probably cringe if you saw the place. Basically it's some old storefront that they converted. Let's not even mention the word sterile. I have boxes of bandages and tape, iodine and rubbing alcohol, and there's a locked drawer if I ever get any real medicine. Once a week this young guy brings in new supplies that he must somehow get from the Outside. Maybe he sneaks it past the National Guard.

Since I started helping people there I've had a few propositions! At least that made me laugh, something I worried I'd left behind outside the concrete walls surrounding us.

*Jess took out all her piercings. Even the tongue bar.
She said they were too modern and interfered with her
studies. She looks a little plainer, but I wouldn't say
that to her face. I think she traded the bar. Ugh. Who
would want that and why?*

Take care. I wish I was there.

Marie

MARIE ADJUSTED THE WHITE DRAPES ALONG THE
metal rods she had spent the past hour installing in the shelter walls.
She had told the others at the shelter they were necessary for patients'
privacy, but that was only a half-truth. She needed them too, to hide
behind in those moments when she felt lost and alone.

Then she would fight back tears by distracting herself with a routine: wiping down the furniture or doing yet another mental checklist
of supplies. Only when everything was in order and there was no one
needing help could she come out from behind the curtains and chat
with the rest of the shelter workers.

She was in the midst of deciding the label for a half-full bottle of
vodka when she heard the latest uproar out front. She ignored the
shouts and wrote the words Hydrogen Peroxide with a fat marker on
surgical tape. Marie was ready to affix the label when she heard her
name called.

The flimsy curtains were suddenly pulled aside and a young man
staggered towards her. The ripped black T-shirt showed a bloody
wound at the shoulder. Small scratches and cuts marred the pale skin
on his neck and lower arm. His black jeans were ripped at the knees.
His face looked familiar, and as he took another step, Marie recognized him as the guy who delivered supplies to the shelter.

Behind him, the other workers seemed ready to engulf him, as
each sought to be the one to help him. He lifted his one fit arm and
waved them back.

Marie moved to assist but the look on his face stopped her, until
his eyes lost their focus and he seemed ready to fall. She let him lean
against her on his good side, and guided him over to sit atop the
metal-topped desk she used as an exam table.

"Close the curtain. I can't—close it so they don't stare." His voice sounded low and tired.

They were all standing right outside, and she gave them a shrug as she pulled the drapes shut.

"They all want a piece of me." He looked drawn, almost stark white, with unruly black hair and dark eyes.

Marie opened a drawer and took out the scissors. "Why?"

As she cut away the tattered remains of the blood-soaked sleeve, she could feel him looking at her. "Because they think I can do anything they want."

"Can you?"

He sucked in a breath as she slowly peeled away the shirt. "So what do you want?"

"You to sit still."

Imbedded in his flesh were slivers of glass, ranging in size from as large as her finger down to small glistening points. "What happened to you?"

"Stained rain." The young man winced as she took a tweezers and started to remove the largest pieces. He saw Marie's confused look. "You haven't been Inside long." He bit his lip a moment. "Stained glass windows are trouble in the Fallen. Tend to shatter whenever a living thing gets near. I was careless around this one temple. As soon as it exploded down on me, I moved."

"Not fast enough." The shards chimed happily as they fell into the metal bowl. Each piece reflected the overhead light like a wet, red jewel.

She spent what felt like hours trying to get all the glass out of him. Towards the end, she had her face only a few inches from his shoulder, muttering that she'd kill for a magnifying glass, as her hand began to cramp trying to lightly tease out every last sliver she could find. Only once did he cry out, when she had to dig the tips of the tweezers down deep. Blood-soaked towels lay at her feet, and she could feel the trails sweat had left down her sides and back.

"I think that's all of them." She reached for the nearby stack of paper napkins and unscrewed the bottle of recently christened peroxide. "This is going to hurt worse than anything."

"Are you always this honest?"

She had to smile at his attitude. Her younger brother had always favored sarcasm as the best form of expression.

Her patient's eyes closed before she began daubing away the blood. His face went another shade paler and his clenched lips trembled. When the wounds were clean, she wrapped them in gauze and tape.

She glanced at the curtains and saw the shadows of the shelter workers gathered behind the cloth. She cursed under her breath and went over to the curtains and pulled them back a few inches.

"Make yourselves useful and find me a clean shirt for him."

Their mad rush as they scattered throughout the shelter to hunt surprised her. Only moments later a little man, no taller than her waist, stumbled over with a worn dress shirt clutched in his hands. He passed it to her as if it were a precious thing, his cramped hands twitching. "Tell Caleb it was me," he said.

Shaking her head, she quickly pulled the curtain closed. Did she even know the little man's name?

"Caleb?"

The young man nodded. "You never told me what you wanted."

Marie felt his hand lightly grip her arm. Instinct wanted her to shake her head and answer him with a muttered "Nothing." But suddenly she was thinking; unbidden, her mind turned back through the last few weeks. The sadness and loneliness, the pain of missing the Jess she had fallen in love with so many months ago, washed over her. Emotions she had fought down and kept at bay in the clinic threatened once more. As the memories went by she realized she was talking, softly, but she couldn't follow what she was saying. It felt like she had woken with the remnants of a dream still drifting about her head.

Caleb let go and frowned. "I'm sorry. I shouldn't have done that. Habit."

Marie didn't understand why he was apologizing. Wasn't she the teary-eyed one who had to turn away a moment and take a few deep breaths to compose herself? She wiped her face with her hands. "You should stay here, at least for tonight."

Caleb shook his head. "That would be wrong for so many reasons." He glanced at the curtain separating them from the rest of the shelter.

"Do you have someplace to go?" She almost offered her place and that unnerved her. How had he managed to bypass her walls?

"Yeah. I'll be back soon so you can give me a second opinion."

She laughed. He tried and winced.

"I don't have anything for pain."

"Don't worry, I'll bring enough for both of us."

Clay,

This is the third time I've tried to write this letter. Why were the others so much easier? I think it's because I don't know how to begin it.

With Jess? Guess I have to, really. Otherwise, if I talk about myself and what's been happening, well, doesn't that really mean I'm not thinking about Jess as much anymore, that she's secondary? I remember when she was all I ever thought about. When I would call her three times during the day just so I could hear her voice.

Now we barely talk. I barely even see her! What to do? Damn, why can't I pick up one of these phones (they're everywhere in the office!) and just call you?

As for me, I'm crying now. Here, I'll wet this with a teardrop on my finger for you to see. Not good. Let's change the subject.

Been spending so much time at the shelter. Last night I even fell asleep there. I woke up later but the workers there wouldn't let me walk home at that hour, so I ended up lying on a cot until the Percocet I took kicked in.

Which brings me to what I almost started this letter with. Caleb. Oh, you would like this boy so much! Remember what you were like in college, the "asshole with a heart"? That's him too. I think he's as lonely as you were then.

Anyway, he's the one that always brings supplies to the shelter, and a few days ago he came in all bloody. Don't ask from what, it would only sound crazy. Like

everything else here does. So I patched him up and,
weirdly, we connected. Yesterday, while I was helping
this little girl who had hair like spun glass (I swear! It
chimed when she moved), he came into the shelter
holding a shopping bag filled with things just for me.
Including the painkillers.

He's Talented. I've talked with the others at the shel-
ter and they tell wild stories about him, not all of them
good. Even though he brings plenty of supplies, they
think he should do more.

Aren't you bored with the film student yet?

Love,

Marie

"SO HOW LONG HAVE YOU BEEN HERE?"
As he walked beside her, Caleb ran his hand along the brick walls
of the buildings they passed. "Inside?" He thought for a moment.
"Maybe since reality Fell away here. I don't even remember what it's
like out there beyond the walls."

He sounded wistful to Marie, and she wondered if even the noto-
rious get lonely.

Up ahead she saw the steps to her building. "Are you sure you
don't want to come up for dinner?"

Caleb shook his head. "Thanks, but I have some rounds to make."
He squeezed her arm good-bye.

Marie watched him walk off, then went inside. She shifted the
bag of leftovers from that evening's meal at the shelter to her other
hand and was about to open the door to their apartment when she
heard the voices: a conversation, coming from behind the thin wood
of the office door. The voices were not clear enough to understood
the words, and she pressed her ear against the door, feeling immediately silly.

Who was inside? Jess home early from a lesson? Had she brought
her teacher back with her? Marie inwardly groaned at the thought of
that revolting man in their home. She opened the door, preparing her-

self for the sight of the anthvoke, but Jess was alone and cradling a moth-worn teddy bear. Marie stumbled a little and her mouth fell open. Which was worse, the fact that Jess wore rags that once were a little girl's sundress, or that the stuffed animal's mouth opened and closed rhythmically, miming every word Jess spoke in a child's falsetto?

Marie couldn't stop herself from shouting. Jess's name, maybe some curses, she wasn't sure exactly what she yelled. The leftovers fell with a soggy thump onto the floor. Jess didn't turn around, didn't drop the bear. She seemed lost in chatter about what kind of ice cream the sky was made out of.

Marie should have been frightened, but a perverse jealousy at seeing how Jess cradled the bear in her arms pushed her onward. A swift grab tore the toy from Jess. Marie was repulsed by the look of the thing, all ratty with one eye, like a corpse of a toy. It even smelled musty. Where had Jess gotten it? The dumpster?

Her lover began to shriek insanely, arms up and clawing at Marie, wanting the bear back. Marie went to the window, the same one all of Jess's new clothes had been tossed from; she opened it and let the bear go.

Jess let out one long wail, then collapsed, crying. Marie dared to go to her, to put her arms around her and try and rock whatever hurt her away. At first Jess fought against her, but soon the struggles quieted and with them most of the tears.

"Why can't you let me have this?"

"It's wrong, so wrong. Can't you see?"

Jess pushed away from Marie and wouldn't look at her. "What's wrong with being different?"

"I don't want you to be different. I love the old Jess."

"I didn't. I hate her." As if to prove it, she made a fist and struck her own thigh.

"Would you rather have the new Jess over me?" Marie asked.

"Do I need to choose?" Jess wiped at the tears on her face.

Marie could not answer her. There seemed nothing left for her to say, so she got up and picked up the leftovers and took them towards the little cubicle in the office that had the refrigerator and the microwave and warmed her dinner. She barely had an appetite.

Clay,

   Jess is asleep in the other room. I think it's after midnight. Even though she's just lying a few feet away she's truly gone. Today I found her... damn, how can I say this? I don't know if she's fucked up her lessons or if all anthvokes are lost in the past, but somehow she's not "here" anymore. Before she collapsed into a deep sleep, I think she called me Holly. Probably a friend from kindergarten.

   I don't know what to do. I feel torn up with guilt for letting her do this to herself.

   I can't compete, especially if this is her heart's desire. There was a time I thought I was.

Marie

THOUGH SHE HAD BEEN AWAKE EVER SINCE THE sunlight found its way through the blinds to shine on her face, Marie stayed next to Jess in the sleeping bag. If she kept her eyes closed and her right arm draped over Jess's chest, then it felt like they still lived together in Philly, off of Lombard Street, and by twelve they'd be heading off to Sisters for that awesome Sunday brunch. But the illusion was not perfect. She could feel the hard floor beneath the sleeping bag, not the pillow top of their mattress. And her fingers were slightly stroking not the soft cotton sleepwear Jess had once favored, but the filmy rags from last night. The two girls that had fallen asleep together nearly every night with one last kiss were long gone.

She knew there was no real point in lying there next to Jess except to torture herself. With a groan, she sat up. She walked down the dimly lit hall to the bathrooms. The electricity didn't work inside— she was never sure where it would work, in the Fallen. Just as well, though. She didn't really want to see her swollen eyes in the mirror. She splashed cold water on her face and then turned the hot faucet. She washed up as best as she could; they had a working shower at the shelter she'd use later on.

Her face still seemed wet after she dried off, and when a salty trickle met her mouth, she realized she had been silently crying without thinking.

She wandered about the office to decide what to take with, but nothing was really hers. All of it belonged to Jess or had been bought for Jess. Except for the letters she had written to Clay, kept on a desk by the dead fax machine. When had she let her life become subsumed in another's? She wiped at her eyes.

She could leave a note, but Jess probably wouldn't even notice it.

On the quiet walk to the shelter she barely looked up from the street. At the glass door, she stopped only because someone stepped in front of her.

"I've been waiting for you."

She blinked and saw Caleb standing there. He wore a smirk along with a tight red-ribbed T-shirt and what had to be the same black jeans as the other day.

"Are you okay?"

He nodded and lightly touched his shoulder. "Better than you, I think." He looked down the street. "Let's take a walk."

Marie followed him.

"I owe you for fixing me up the other day."

She was about to speak, but he held up a hand to quiet her. "No, listen first, then you can tell me what you think." He stopped and looked around some more, acting secretive.

He even whispered, though no one else was around. "Would you like me to get you out of here?"

"What?"

"Shhh. I can get you past the walls. It won't be easy, but you seem miserable here because of Jess. So I'm offering you an out."

She stepped back, felt the hard brick wall against her. Lots of the people who came to the shelter griped about being trapped in the Fallen Area. Most truly were. The ones changed by the Fall, the Afflicted and those that had developed their Talents, couldn't survive long Outside. The rest—well, once you decided to enter through the barbed wire and immense walls surrounding the city, the guards at the gate would prevent your return. Still, the thought of returning home was intoxicating.

But she found herself saying "No."

Caleb looked at her, but his reaction was unreadable.

"I can't leave her." She looked back in the direction of the office they shared. How could she have thought about deserting Jess? She felt on fire, angry with herself, terribly ashamed. "I need to go back."

"Let me come with you, then. I may be able to help with Jess."

"How do you know her?" Suspicion suddenly ran through her. They all said Caleb was Talented. Was he a friend of the anthvoke's?

"Relax. I only found out about her through you."

Marie rubbed at her face. "I told you?" She began to remember that moment at the shelter with Caleb when she had mumbled things to him.

He nodded. "Sort of. Anyway, maybe together we can reach her." He took hold of her hand and squeezed. "I think she'd come around if she realized what she's losing."

Together they headed back, stopping at the shelter door. Through the glass she saw the usual crowd of misfits, refugees, and normals within.

"It's this way." Marie pointed down the block.

"My way is quicker." He took hold of the door handle. When he opened it, she saw not the shelter's interior but the office. Across the room, Jess still lay sleeping.

"How?" She leaned on the doorjamb, feeling lost.

Caleb grinned. "Not everyone in the Fallen will hurt you, Marie."

She remembered that he was Talented. But all her hesitation began to fall away—if there was any chance Jess could be returned to her... She followed Caleb in.

"There are two things I can do. I can open her eyes to your feelings and make her more aware of them. Hopefully she'll realize she's hurting you and come back to you."

"And the second choice?"

Caleb looked away from her. "It's cruel. I open her heart to you. Metaphysically. Forces her to fall in love with you, to ache for you." He shook his head slowly. "But I doubt it's really true love."

The thought horrified Marie. "No, not that way." If opening Jess's eyes failed, it might well mean that she never had really loved Marie, at least not enough to matter.

"Wake her up."

Marie knelt down beside the slumbering figure and lightly kissed her ear. The faint scents of sweat and body odor drifted from Jess, and Marie wondered when she'd last taken a shower. Jess had once seemed to Marie an "incorruptible," always giving off a sweet smell.

"Jess." She gently shook her by the arm.

The sleeper began to stir, first moving her lips a little, and then opening her delicate eyelashes.

"Marie?" Jess looked surprised to see her there. Had her dreams somehow picked up on Marie's decision to abandon her only an hour or so ago?

"Hey, sweetheart." Marie pointed at Caleb, who had sat down next to them. "This is a friend. He's going to help us."

"Help us what? Are we missing something?" Jess yawned, a single strand of silvery saliva breaking apart on her lips.

"Yes. We are." And it all became so clear and yet more complicated. They both were missing each other, had gone astray. Not just Jess. When had Marie stopped understanding, stopped knowing what Jess was thinking? Maybe months ago, before they even set foot inside the Fallen Area.

Marie turned to Caleb. "You have to do us both."

"What?"

"Open my eyes, too." She took Jess's hand in her own, weaving together their fingers in a welcome and familiar pattern. "I need to know why she wanted to come here. I need to know her again, as much as I want her to see me."

Caleb's brow creased, and for a moment it made him look years older. Marie had to wonder what his real age was.

Jess seemed to notice him for the first time, her eyes narrowing. "Wait a sec, you're Talen—"

Caleb made a hushing sound and lifted both his hands, fingers spread wide apart. He waved his hands once before their faces, and that was all it took. Marie felt her head jerk slightly, her neck stiffen, as if unseen hands held her rigid. Her eyes widened to the verge of pain, but she saw nothing but blackness. For a moment . . .

. . . their old apartment. Not cozy anymore, but stifling, with walls that were taller than she had ever noticed. Each one seemed so close.

And everything seemed dull; the colors long since faded, with no shine whatsoever.

She looked at the wall clock, which had a face so distorted she had to stare to read it. The twelve and the six were swollen out of proportion, leaving the other numbers almost unseen.

Where was she? Her hand lifted the television remote and she noticed that her lavender nail polish had started to chip. Once that would have sent her scurrying to the bedroom and to that drawer filled with bottles of every shade imaginable. But now she could only stare at the flawed edge and wonder if it even mattered how she looked. Her finger tapped the button on the remote and the television came to life. But she didn't bother to watch, could not hear anything. Why bother? Her gaze went back to the clock, waiting for the hands to reach six o'clock, when Marie would come back to her.

. . . the round table too small to seat three. A fat candle burned. On her right sat her lover. Marie seemed distracted, reading the autographs on the black and white photographs on the restaurant wall.

The other woman next to them shuffled a deck of cards. The backs of the tarot cards were decorated with Egyptian pyramids and a scraggly-looking camel. The first cards were laid down and though the woman's mouth moved, she couldn't hear a single word. No matter. The cards held her interest, not what was said. The urge to reach out and feel them, to touch the woman who struggled with an armful of swords, was nearly overwhelming. She glanced back at Marie, who smiled at her—a patient smile, she knew, but it had the same effect as all her different smiles: a sense of calm, of reassurance, came over her. Even though Marie did not believe in tarot or crystals or psychic hotlines, she believed in her. Soon cards covered the tabletop, arranged in an odd pattern that she wished she understood. They teased her with their pictures and exotic names. When was the last time anyone used the word Hierophant? Why didn't she know what it meant?

. . . the chamber was cramped, every space filled with things. So many wonderful old things. She wanted to explore the shop and all its treasures inch by inch but it was time for her lesson to begin.

She carefully made her way through to the back, which had been cleared for her studies. Darkness. That had been the first test, a few days ago, to evoke light. Now reaching out, not with her hands—that wouldn't have worked, as most of the lamps were broken—but with something within her. To find the lava lamps spaced around the room and bring them back to life was simple, and yet felt just as thrilling as the first time she had set them aglow. The light revealed a new challenge on the floor.

An old telephone, black Bakelite handle, cloth-covered cord broken and frayed at the end. She knelt down in front of it, hesitated, and gave herself a moment to breathe deeply. A broken fingernail tapped the metal rotary dial. With her other hand she lifted the receiver. It felt heavy to her touch, different from all the cheap plastic phones she had held in the past. Different but somehow right. She brought it to her face and mouthed the ʼword "Hello" again and again. She closed her eyes and envisioned a spread of warmth flowing from her chest, up her throat, past her lips into the receiver. Her teeth began to ache, but then came the reward of a dial tone. Her eyes flew open and she gasped in pleasure. Who to call? Who to share this joy, this sense of magic with? Her first thought, as it often was, was Marie. The dial began to move, turning of its own accord, and she heard the line ring. An automatic voice answered, the name of some realty company. The office. The empty office. She slowly put the phone down. Marie wasn't there, not there to share with her. . . .

Her eyes suddenly felt raw and dry, and she blinked with relief at finally being able to close her heavy lids. When she could see clearly again, her first sight was Jess crying, soft sobs that lightly shook her. Caleb let out a breath and collapsed backwards to the floor, his lips parted as he gasped for small breaths.

There was a tug on her hand, and she remembered that Jess and she were still holding onto each other. Jess brought their hands to her face and rubbed them over her wet eyes then down to her mouth and lips. She whispered words, and Marie moved closer to hear them. "I'm sorry, I'm so sorry."

Then they were kissing, and, for a moment, breathless.

She found Caleb standing by the front door. He looked tired. She wanted to speak, to offer the perfect "thank you" and let him know how much it meant to have her love back. But even calm, she would never be able to express everything in words, and so she just wrapped her arms around him and put her head on his lean chest. She felt him return the hug with a squeeze.

"I'll tell the shelter that you won't be coming in today."

She let him go and watched as he opened the door. Beyond she saw the street three floors below them. He nodded good-bye and left them alone.

Clay,

We're together! We're together! Part of me wants to sing and another part to cry. Happy tears, though. I can't tell you know how it happened, I need to think, let it all sink in. All I know is that months ago Jess and I had been growing apart. She was miserable, feeling lost, alone, and worthless. She needed to feel special, not from me but from within. That's why she came to the Fallen, to be something. Not to leave me behind.

I know now she has always thought of me, loved me.

Last night she went with me to the shelter and helped out. It was amazing. They have this old coffeepot in the back, and thanks to Jess it works now. Unlimited free java! She basked in their thanks. I think she finally realizes that to feel special she had to start from within. We came home and made love for hours, and fell asleep entwined.

We're going to take a morning walk, but I wanted to write you that everything's turned around. I'd forgotten what hope felt like. I would put this letter with the others, 'cept I don't know where they disappeared to. Maybe this office is haunted. If so, well, the ghosts got an eyeful last night!

Love... yes, I'm in love.

Marie

MARIE STEPPED OUTSIDE INTO THE WARM sunlight and found Caleb sitting on the sidewalk outside the office building. He smiled up at her and held up a chocolate bar. "I brought gifts."

Marie practically purred and sat down beside him. "Jess and I were hoping to see you tonight." She took the offered candy and quickly tore away the foil wrapping. She could resist the smell for only a few seconds, but she held back to just a nibble. Like a drug, the seductive taste of rich chocolate evoked emotions: happiness at having something sweet melting in her mouth, followed quickly by a little guilt—she didn't really need all the calories. She looked at the candy and sighed. Why did she always become so attached to things that were bad for her?

"That's supposed to make you happy."

"It does." But she couldn't sound enthusiastic. "Maybe you could make me see how wrong it is to eat this."

He laughed. "Maybe."

She took another bite, bringing a sweet shrouded almond into her mouth and sucking away the chocolate surrounding it. "By the way, I've been curious."

"Yes?"

"Remember plan B, opening the heart? Have you ever done that? Made someone love you?"

Caleb softly muttered, "A few times." He looked down at his worn sneakers and slumped his body forward a little.

She instantly felt bad that she'd brought the subject up. "You said gifts. What else did you bring?"

"Yeah." Caleb reached into the pocket of his jeans and brought out a piece of folded stationery.

Marie opened it along the first crease, careful not to smudge it with melted chocolate, and saw the familiar blue ink and Clay's unmistakable long cursive script.

"You took the letters!"

He nodded. "I think he was surprised that you bothered to write them."

Her heart skipped in her chest. This boy had returned everything to her—the love of her friend, the love of her partner—he truly could do anything. She gave him a kiss on the cheek, leaving behind a little sugary imprint on the pale skin.

"We've been thinking about you." Both looked up to see Jess standing just outside the lobby door. She smoothed out the waist of the brown velveteen dress she wore, and then slowly walked down the steps. She leaned down and kissed the top of Marie's head. "We've been thinking of a way to reward you." Marie nodded. "Wasn't easy deciding what to get."

"Wait a sec, you don't have to—"

"Shhh, too late." Jess reached into the small purse at her side and pulled out something small with curving metal lines. Marie took hold of Caleb's hands, cupping them together so that Jess could set the antique spectacles on his palms. The metal ends of the frames curled up like the legs of some spindly insect, and the glass lenses caught the warm reflection of the afternoon sun.

"Since you opened our eyes," Marie said, "we thought this was sort of fitting."

Jess moved closer against Marie, slipping her arm around her shoulder. "They're British. From 1910." Almost as if it were a side thought, she added, "Clay likes men in glasses."

Dearest Marie,

What to say? Here I have been thinking you were lost forever, and these letters show up through my mail slot.

I read every word you wrote. The words reached deep within me, and after each letter I found myself wishing I could be there by your side. Of course, this whole Fallen business sounds dreadful, so perhaps it is best that I was a comfort in spirit.

I am left with, what to say? I am relieved and thrilled that Jess is yours once more. If only my dalliance with the film student had lasted as long as your time of trial. I envy the love you two share, and will hold it in mind on my next romantic encounter.

Fate willing (or should I make that Fallen willing?), I will hear from you again. I trust that the same agent that brought me your letters will convey mine to you.

Your dearest friend indeed,

Clayton

HAIR LIKE FIRE,
BLOOD LIKE SILK

"HUNGRY?"

Zane looked up to see the crude reflection of the young man who'd spoken. In the grimy windows of the restaurant he had been eyeing hungrily for the past hour, the figure cautiously approached where Zane sat on the curb.

Zane was surprised when he glanced back over his shoulder. Though the clothes were mismatched—worn jeans, a faded T-shirt peeking through the rips in a pullover—the body beneath them was perfect: the full torso of an athlete, with strong limbs and rich brown skin. And the face had chiseled cheekbones and a wide nose.

The stranger nodded towards the window and spoke again. "Want to go inside?"

Zane shook his head, brushing aside several locks of long red hair that fell into his blue eyes. "No cash." He lacked even a wallet. On his first night inside the Fallen Area, a pack of guys had jumped him— they threw him against a wall and started kicking him when he fell, their dirty sneakers vicious against his stomach and legs. Then they'd taken everything of worth from him, even a cheap watch.

The young man—who couldn't have been much older than Zane, maybe twenty at most—smiled, showing rows of white teeth. "Don't need any. C'mon." He opened the thick wooden door and went inside.

Zane hesitated a moment. After the mugging, he didn't think he could trust anyone Inside anymore, but his stomach lurched at the thought of finally eating something—yesterday morning he had found himself staring at a pigeon pecking at a scrap of bread on the sidewalk, and feeling almost envious of the bird.

The restaurant was one long room in complete disarray. The few people eating sat on salvaged church pews. Zane glanced at the windows, curious whether they were stained glass, but they gaped empty except for some crumbling mortar.

Zane followed the other boy to an empty pew. They sat down near the end of the pew, a few feet apart. As soon as Zane leaned back against the scarred wood, the weariness he'd been fending off took over. He didn't remember closing his eyes, but a firm shake of his shoulder roused him.

"Let me guess. First night in the Fallen?"

Zane hesitated before answering. The other boy had moved nearer on the pew, was now only inches away. Zane was too tired to really care. "No. Third." The word came out in a cranky tone, and was followed by a yawn.

The other boy nodded absently.

The smell of food intensified as a rough squeal heralded a push-cart loaded with pots and plates. The man who pushed it looked every bit like a beast of burden: low to the ground and squat, arms and legs thick and heavily furred, and a flat flushed face lost between wide ears. He wheezed and whistled as he approached the two young men.

"Saj, you're back," the large man said to the brown-skinned guy. "What's this, twice this week? I think you like my food after all."

Saj shrugged and grinned. "It's easier than catching a meal."

The man laughed, a rough sound that culminated in a wet cough, and abruptly removed the nearest lid. Steam rose up from whatever simmered inside, carrying the smell of spices to them.

Zane watched as Saj reached for a bowl from the cart. He took a chipped ceramic bowl for his own share. The man ladled out generous helpings. Each dripped brown and greasy, but Zane didn't care. It smelled like actual food.

"Henry, this makes us even from last time."

The man narrowed already tiny eyes at Saj for a moment, then shrugged. "Fine, whatever." He then turned to Zane. "Pay up." Henry held out a meaty hand. The wrinkles and creases were outlined with dirt. Or maybe the dried remains of the stew.

"I—I thought..." Zane turned to Saj, panic rising in his chest. "You said I didn't need cash."

Henry chuckled, which brought up some loose phlegm that nearly choked the man.

Saj slid down the pew away from Zane. "Well, I meant to tell you that Henry here doesn't take cash—not everyone Inside does. But you seemed so slick, after spending, what, three days here. I figured you were savvy and knew how everything's played."

Zane groaned. "All right, I'm sorry for being an asshole." He looked back up at the immense man. "What do you want for it?" Immediately he regretted asking; Henry eyed him intently. Zane wasn't that hungry.

"It's a small bowl. Hmmm. How about two snips?" Henry's bloated fingers made a scissoring motion.

Zane paled in confusion.

"He wants some of your hair," said Saj. He looked amused.

"Oh." Zane instinctively brushed his fingers across his forehead, but his hair for once had stayed out of his eyes. He nearly chuckled at the weird request, but Henry's constant stare made him inwardly shudder. "Okay."

The chef rummaged around on the crowded cart for a moment before lifting up a wicked-looking pair of scissors, the jagged-bladed variety used to cut bones. Zane shut his eyes tightly, waiting. He started to count to himself to keep calm, and on fifteen felt a slight tug.

An audible snip, then another.

When Zane opened his eyes, Henry's fat lips grinned at the two locks of hair he held in his left hand. He pushed a few strands to the edge of his fingers and blew lightly. The hair flew off and a flash of fire erupted in the air. Zane blinked wildly, shocked that his face wasn't singed.

"Love red hair," Henry muttered. He pushed his cart away towards his next customer.

A black sky loomed overhead when they left the restaurant. Zane had trouble walking. His eyes felt as heavy as his feet, and he realized that tonight he would not be able to stay awake as he'd struggled to do the past few nights.

Saj gently laid a hand on his shoulder. "You need a place to stay?"

"Yeah," Zane murmured.

"Come back with me."

Zane groggily nodded. During the past couple of nights he had slept for only a few hours, when he could no longer stay awake, in a doorway near the gates to the Fallen Area. The thought of a safe place to collapse became irresistible.

Saj lived on the top floor of a not-too-distant building. Zane rested his head against the elevator wall. The elevator seemed to have too many buttons, and most of them had weird lettering instead of numbers.

The sliding doors opened on a dim hall. Zane trudged along after Saj, thankful when they stopped at an apartment door. Saj smiled at him as he turned a key in the lock. Inside, a bare bulb hung from the ceiling and flickered annoyingly. A mattress on the floor, layers of colorful blankets, and lots of pillows kept the front room from being empty. Cracks in the graying plaster decorated the bare walls.

Saj pointed across the room at a far door. "There's the bathroom. The rest I wouldn't bother with." He began pulling off clothes: first the sweater, then the shirt underneath. Bare-chested, he hesitated a moment in front of Zane, who blushed deeply and turned his head to stare out the window.

"I'm going to take a shower," he heard Saj call out. A moment later the door closed, and soon the soothing sound of water running filled the apartment.

Zane sank to his knees amid all the pillows with a sigh. The memory of a shirtless Saj, with his perfect, smooth, muscular chest, stayed with him, making it even easier to relax in bed. He was asleep soon after laying his head down.

Zane stirred awake when he felt the mattress sag under the other's weight. Saj's bare skin gave off a cool and fresh aura. "Can I touch you?" he whispered in Zane's ear. Zane struggled to keep his eyes open, and lightly grunted, sleepily rolling over onto his back so his body brushed against Saj. He shivered when a cool hand slipped underneath his T-shirt and began stroking his stomach. But though part of him was stirring, by the time the wet kisses began on his neck, he was falling asleep again.

Afternoon light reached Zane's eyes, turning his dreams to shades of amber and then red. He blinked away sleep and stretched, his arm narrowly missing the naked boy wrapped around him. He stopped moving and remembered last night, how he came to be lying there, in a stranger's room, lying next to a young man with skin that looked like warm chocolate.

Zane touched Saj's bare arm, and sure enough, the skin felt warm. His fingers went up along the arm, over the smooth shoulder and down to the boy's chest, until they circled the few dark hairs that surrounded Saj's nipple. Zane marveled at how his hand had taken a direction of its own, possessed by a need to explore new territory, and he started to smile.

Then Saj's eyes opened, and Zane jumped a little, bringing his hand up to his mouth as if the fingertips were singed. "Morning."

Zane brought up his legs and rested his chin on his knees. "Hey." He felt flushed, embarrassed, and excited, all in one dizzying mix.

"Sleep okay?"

He nodded. "Thanks for letting me spend the night." He sniffed away some morning congestion and rubbed his face.

"No prob." Saj slipped his hand between the bent legs, so his fingers were at the edge of the boxers Zane wore. Both became very still. Then Saj's fingertips began to venture into the leg of the boxers, gently sliding up the thigh.

Zane closed his eyes. Once he had been at a rave, lying in a sweaty puddle of other kids. One boy had leaned over and, as the DJ moved the electric sounds around the speakers, Zane had realized they were kissing. He almost stopped, but it felt really good to work his mouth around the other's tongue. The X, he told himself. Only when the girls he had come to the rave with started to giggle and drape their candy-colored beads around his head did he stop. They'd teased him for the rest of the school year.

Now a guy was touching him. Really touching him. The sensation of the fingers slowly moving over his trembling skin was heady, like a shot of nitrous. Zane's breath caught in his chest and he remained still except for the occasional shudder as Saj continued to explore until finally he began stroking Zane's hard dick. Saj's eyes, round and brown, drank in Zane's gaze. The speed of the touch began to quicken, and Zane found himself groaning; he clenched his teeth together, ashamed at hearing his voice so weak and needy. But that could not stop the rush, and without thinking, he spread his legs more and began to rock slightly, back and forth, in time with the rhythm kept by Saj's hand. When he came, each nerve sent scrambled signals like an epileptic fit, and his body shook as he shot white strands all over the other boy's arm and the covers beneath them.

Zane collapsed back onto the covers and absently covered his face with one bent arm. He couldn't bring his mind to relax; could not even think. It took all his effort to calm down, listen to his racing heartbeat. The sound of Saj rising for the bathroom, the rush of water as the toilet flushed were so mundane they brought his thoughts back to where he was. Zane moved his arm aside and saw the older boy, now wearing faded boxers, sit down on the bare floorboards not far from him.

Something shiny flashed in his hand. A razor blade, the old fashioned double-edged kind.

"What are you doing?"

Saj looked at him suddenly, as if startled. "Oh, don't worry... it's for me. I—I have to come down."

Nervous curiosity made Zane slide a little closer to Saj, and he noticed for the first time all the pale lines that crisscrossed the other boy's hands and forearms. How had he missed them before?

"Come down?"

Saj nodded. He lightly laid one edge of the razor blade against the back of his left hand. "Yeah... whenever I get too excited, too emotional...," he said in a hushed voice. "Well, if I cut myself, it brings me back down."

Zane felt himself blush. "I made you excited?" It seemed so odd for Saj to say, if only because Zane was the one that had been taken over the edge.

Saj grinned again, that wonderful smile. "Yeah. And, well, happy too."

Zane watched with utter fascination as the young man's fingers moved fast and the blade bit lightly into the dark skin to leave a thin red line. Zane held his breath as the blood started to fall. Not in drops, but as a thin long stream. When it reached the floor, it pooled a moment, then began to scuttle, dragging from what had become a small plump red thorax and abdomen a thread of blood still connected to Saj's hand. Zane leapt to his feet and backed away, heart pounding.

"Don't be scared," Saj said. With almost routine skill, his other hand broke the slender thread. The wound was already closing. The crimson spider rushed off to disappear into the shadows in a corner of the room.

"I—I heard things happen Inside." Zane looked down at the young man and slowly shook his head. He looked so normal, but this...

"It's okay. I'm okay." Saj spoke slowly, calmly. "Things do happen here." He rose up in a smooth, graceful motion. Hiding the cut arm behind him, he moved to where Zane stood by the window.

"Do you want to stay in or go out with me today?"

Zane caught himself thinking how normal Saj looked on the outside. More than normal, beautiful. Glad to talk about something else, the younger boy shrugged. "What will you be doing?"

"Work. I scavenge for things to sell." With a regretful sigh, Saj headed towards a battered chest of drawers set against the wall. He began to rummage through the clothes. "Sometimes you can find some cool things." He found a T-shirt with cut-off sleeves and pulled it on, then grabbed some torn blue jeans. "I never wear new clothes to work."

"Like what's some of the stuff you've found?"

Saj closed a drawer and thought for a moment, casually leaning against the cheap furniture. "Fur coats—bitch to carry, but lots of folk like to sleep on them. Sporting goods are always in demand. I once found an old telephone that an anthvoke paid me big money for."

Zane had never heard of an anthvoke, but suddenly he found himself asking, "Anything to drink or pop?"

Saj furrowed his brow, which made him look years older. "You mean liquor or pills, right?"

Zane nodded. He couldn't tell if Saj was cool with him asking.

Saj nudged him with a bare foot. "If you really want that stuff, well, we can try a pharmacy, but they were the first sites cleaned out after the Fall. Might have to love being dry for a while."

Zane reached for the clothes he had worn yesterday and the day before and the day before that. He took a tentative sniff and wrinkled his face. That meant he probably smelled just as bad. "Can I take a shower before we go?"

When he came out of the Spartan bathroom with a spare towel around his waist, he found his clothes gone. He could feel Saj looking him over. He felt awkward standing there, unsure what he should do.

"I think those will fit you," Saj said with a nod towards the dresser. Atop it was a neatly folded pile. Saj sat near the front door, lacing up his sneakers. A beat-up backpack swung over his shoulder. Against the wall leaned a golf club.

Zane picked up the clothes. A gray T-shirt and sweat shorts and blue designer boxers. "Thanks."

Saj didn't answer, just grinned at him. That only made Zane all the more uneasy. How could the guy act so comfortable around Zane, like they were old friends? He couldn't bring himself to drop the towel there in the same room, and felt his face burning as he took the offered clothes back with him to the bathroom and changed.

Zane didn't really pay attention to where they were going; he just followed Saj as they went down one street, crossed over to the next. They passed dozens of buildings, most of them looking abandoned or decaying.

"No one ever drives?" He hadn't seen a running car since entering the Fallen, just forgotten heaps lying either in the street or on the sidewalk. He had nearly slept in a battered Honda the first night, but something large and scaly had slithered under the seat when he'd opened the door.

"Nah. Gas is too expensive and all that technology is just begging to be messed."

Saj had brought the golf club along with him. He raised the end and pointed down an alley on their right. Someone had spraypainted graffiti on the nearest wall.

"So who's Moil?"

"It's a warning, not a name. There are others, but that's the easiest to remember. Just don't go down there."

Like he would just wander down strange alleys anyway? Still, he was curious what was so dangerous down there. All he could see were piles of refuse.

"Heap."

"What?"

"I think there's a heap down there—at least, that's what we call them. Something big and real nasty amid all the crap and trash that just swallows you up."

Zane gave a nervous chuckle but felt better only when they were far from the alley. "So where are we going?"

"What you said earlier made me remember this one place filled with doctors' offices, not that far from here." Saj glanced around, as if to get his bearings. "I think it's been untouched since the Fall."

"Cool." Zane remembered one classmate in the high school he had abandoned whose father was an allergist or something. She always came to raves with some new colorful pill to share.

The glass front doors of the building had long ago been shattered. Nasty shards, all encrusted with grime, framed the way inside. Saj went through first, lightly tapping the floors, then the walls, with the golf club. He nodded at Zane to come in.

"Caution's your best friend."

Zane scowled slightly behind Saj's back. His father used that same tone, especially after the first scotch and soda of the evening, and it always bothered Zane. No matter what the words were, the meaning was simple and clear: that Zane was nothing more than a child. He fought down the memory and went over to the far wall, on which hung an encased directory of all fifteen floors. He tapped at the plastic shield covering the letters. A few fell from the board like dead insects.

"Looks like there are a lot of doctors here," he muttered, needing to say something.

"Were. I doubt any survived." Saj headed around the lobby corner. "Here are the elevators," he called out. "All dead.... Found the stairs," he added. "Anything on the second or third floor?"

Zane scanned the board. "Nope. What's rheumatology?"

"Muscles and bones, I think," Saj answered absently.

"There's a doc of that on the fifth floor. That's the first one."

"Shit," Saj said.

Zane walked over to where Saj stood by the stairwell door. He looked through the small wired-glass panel but could see nothing beyond but darkness. Saj unslung and unzipped his backpack, reaching in for a flashlight, one of the mean-looking plastic ones wrapped in thick rubber. "Hope you don't mind climbing a few flights."

"'Sokay."

Saj led the way, letting Zane carry the golf club. The lonely flashlight beam illuminated the empty stairs. The door shutting behind them echoed, far too ominous for Zane's comfort.

Saj paused at the first landing. "You see anything move, tell me," he whispered. "If it's within reach, smash it."

Close together, they moved slowly and carefully, trying to be silent. The air in the stairwell hung hot and stale, and by the time they reached the third flight, both had broken a sweat. At the fifth landing, Zane watched and held his breath as Saj checked first the door, then the hall, which was, oddly, not as dark as the others. After a right turn, then a left, they saw a faint light coming down the corridor from beneath a far door.

"Damn," Saj said under his breath, and shook his head. "I should have figured."

"What is it?" Zane whispered, his face so close that his lips were practically touching the other young man's smooth cheek. It made him shiver on the inside, and he wished he could just bring himself to lean in a little more and kiss him.

"I don't know." Saj absently reached out and squeezed Zane's shoulder comfortingly.

There was enough light to make out the sign on the door. Sure enough, it was the rheumatologist. Saj pressed his ear to the door a moment, then tried the handle. Unlocked, it turned easily, and the bluish light that spilled out blinded them for a moment. Beyond, they glimpsed the waiting room, the window to the receptionist area, and another door, ajar, that led deeper into the office. The overhead panels were dark, and whatever illuminated the area flickered slightly.

Zane watched from the doorway as Saj stepped in, turned to the right, and then stepped back in shock. He muttered something, too quiet for the younger boy to hear, and his expression held a mix of disgust and sadness.

"What?" Zane hesitated another second then went in.

People sat in the waiting room. Not many; he counted five: two old ladies sitting next to each other, engrossed in the magazines on their laps; a young mother watching her toddler wander around the floor; and a middle-aged man, who seemed ready to fall asleep. Not one looked up to notice Saj and Zane standing there. All of them were bathed in that spooky light, not from the lamps on the table but emanating from and surrounding the metal and vinyl chairs, the end tables, and the bored people.

Zane took a step towards them. Saj reached out for him but was too late to prevent him from walking into solid air. He struck with not enough force to hurt, but the impact shook him.

"What the fuck?" Zane reached out and his hand met a smooth barrier, invisible to the eye. His fingers felt a tingle like static electricity, and the fine red hairs on the back of his hand and along his forearm stood up and took notice. The people on the other side continued with their tedium. "It's like they're on television." Zane stroked the air, feeling the expanse of the wall.

"Must have happened with the Fall." Saj had already moved to the receptionist's window and was glancing in.

"You mean they've been in there since then? Shit." The thought of being trapped like that forever made him shudder.

Saj shrugged. "There's nothing we can do. Leave them." He had already walked over to the other door. "Let's get what we came for."

The rest of the office was in darkness, and the farther they moved from the waiting room, the more dependent they were on the flashlight. Along the hallway were examination rooms.

Zane felt on edge, peering back behind him towards the waiting room; though they were out of sight, he knew those people were still back there, trapped, and it unnerved him. The air seemed worse than the stairwell's, so heavy and oppressive that the sweat-soaked shirt he wore felt like thick wool.

Saj found a supply closet filled with drug samples. "Keep watch." He opened his backpack and began to check out the many bottles and packets, choosing some to throw into the bag. The rest were relegated to the closet floor.

Beads of sweat rolled into Zane's eyes, burning his vision. He lifted an arm to wipe his sight clear, and thought he saw something pitch black move, far down the hall. He squinted, still feeling the salt sting, and waited, and saw something shift, as if one of the shadows had moved an inch or two closer.

"Saj. Something's here," he hissed.

The other boy stopped and shone the flashlight down the corridor. Nothing in the beam. "What did it look like?"

"I don't know. It was black, along the wall and hard to see. You're the fucking expert." An edge of hysteria crept into his whisper.

"Shit. Like I thought."

He suddenly took Zane by the arm and pulled him through the doorway of the nearest empty examination room, then shut the door behind them and turned the lock.

"Help me," he said and began opening all the cabinets and drawers. "Grab all the bottles of rubbing alcohol."

Zane did as he was told, hearing the urgency in Saj's voice. He felt a measure of relief that there was something he could do, a simple task that did not require him to think and remember how confused he was.

Saj picked up a bottle, unscrewed the cap and emptied it over Zane's head.

"Hey! What the fuck?" He regretted crying out, but the alcohol on his skin and hair had chilled him like a sudden ice bath.

"We have to pour all of this over ourselves." Saj had already opened the next bottle. "Trust me."

Zane shivered when more alcohol spilled over him, splashing down his shirt, dripping over his arms. A weird calm settled over him, like a child watching others rush around but feeling distant and apart from them, lost in the observation. He looked at Saj, who frantically drenched him. Then Saj said, "I need you." The numbness changed to real fear. Zane grabbed the nearest bottle, twisted off the cap and began wetting down Saj. A harsh, medicinal smell clung to both of them like a thick aura.

Zane saw the thing's claw first. It slipped through the crack between door and frame, resembling a blackened, shriveled leaf twitching in the wind. It slid through, scratching, finally reaching up and clutching the knob and unlocking the door.

The thing swept into the room then, a mass of black moth wings fluttering madly. No real body, nothing resembling a head, simply countless arms ending in sharp spindle claws that raked the air. It rushed at Zane, who screamed, lifting his arms to shield his face and chest, the nine-iron he held forgotten.

"Don't panic. Alcohol's poison to it." But even Saj's voice trembled.

Zane expected the pain of countless claws slashing his flesh but felt only the cool sensation of the alcohol drying on his skin. He brought down his arms and saw that the creature had backed up against the wall, pushing forward only to occasionally claw at Saj, but its talons stopped inches away from him.

Saj meanwhile dropped the flashlight on the exam bed and grabbed the golf club from Zane's loose grip. He swung, not at the thing, but behind him at the wall. Zane was sure that the older boy had gone crazy until he saw the target: an oddly shaped bin labeled "Medical Waste" and bolted to the wall.

His face twisted with the effort, Saj hit the bin twice more. All the while the creature fluttered madly about. The hard plastic finally cracked and out poured a shower of used needles, stained gauze, and soiled latex.

The creature swooped down on the waste, eagerly enveloping it with all its arms.

Saj grabbed the flashlight and shouted to Zane, "Run!"

The two scrambled, not looking back at the creature in the room, at the people trapped forever in the waiting area, or down the hall when they reached the stairway door. They ran down each flight of steps, not slowing until they hurled themselves at the ground floor door, out into the lobby and back into sunshine and the street outside.

"What was that thing?" Zane gasped between breaths.

"A fect." Saj sat down on the sidewalk. "If it touched you, that would be the end." He also panted heavily, but began sorting through the rewards of the day. "Cancer, HIV, bubonic plague. Whatever." He lifted up one paper box of pills, shook it, and was rewarded by a satisfying rattle, then dropped it back in his pack. "It's the ultimate carrier. Some sorta sickness ghost."

"Shit. I mean, ... shit. And you do this every day?"

To Zane, Saj's responding grin looked wild and thrilling.

Zane followed after Saj, merrily rolling over and over in his head such strange-sounding names as Hyalgan and Enbrel. After they had looked over their loot, he had pleaded to try one of the brightly colored pills, but Saj insisted that a doped boy walking through the Fallen streets was not a good thing. Rather than be sullen, Zane consoled himself with the thought of sorting through drugs at home like Halloween candy. And taking a shower to rid himself of the stink of the alcohol. He sniffed his fingertips, wincing at the smell that lingered on his skin.

Back in the apartment building, Saj walked past the elevator and the stairs, headed for the rear of the building. Zane paused by the elevator doors.

"Where are you going?"

"To Nifty's. She's my fence," Saj called over his shoulder. "She buys the stuff I find."

"Oh. She lives in the same building?"

Saj shook his head. "Come on."

Zane found Saj waiting for him around the corner, standing in front of a small door. Shoddy gilded letters on the frosty glass pane read "Broom Closet." "Ummm, we're hiding the stuff?"

"Nope." Saj reached for the knob. "This is the way."

"Through a broom closet?"

The older boy opened the door to the tiniest of spaces—enough to hold a bristly broom, a dirty old mop and bucket, and a few brushes hanging from rusty pegs along the wall. Zane almost laughed, but Saj seemed so serious that he felt a little uneasy.

"Nifty's just past all the broom closets in the Fallen." He took a step into the closet, pushing aside the mop. "They have to be old, I mean, really say 'broom closet' and not anything janitorial."

"Wait a sec," Zane said, reaching for Saj's shoulder but his fingers closed over empty air. Saj had, impossibly, moved deeper into the closet. He had passed the brushes and was now behind the broom and still walking. And then he was gone, utterly swallowed up.

Zane reached out and touched the mop handle. The wood felt solid enough. Still, he shuddered. This reminded him of the people trapped back at the doctor's office, stretching belief past sanity. Blood spiders and fiery hair could have a place in this new world for Zane, but to ask him to step through on blind trust was almost too much to bear. He suddenly had the urge to collapse, to sit down on the floor and close his eyes. He needed some serious down-time, a chance to relax, to ease into the madness of the Fallen slowly. But there wasn't time for that.

Days ago, at the gate, as the clerk was destroying his citizenship, Zane had experienced a moment of panic. He almost stopped the man from cutting up his Social Security card, his old identity, scared of where what seemed at the time a whim had brought him. He looked at the others in line to enter the Fallen, an assortment of the physically abused, the emotionally battered, the needy, and the lost, and realized that the normal world offered them as little as it had offered him.

Zane leaned against the doorjamb, readying himself. "Only another gate," he whispered. Saj had kept him alive, and deserved his trust. He closed his eyes, counted to ten, and finally began to walk ahead. He expected something, some sensation, but felt nothing, not even the slightest tingle. Just the old tiled floor to meet his feet. After daring a few more steps to be sure, he opened his eyes.

He found himself standing beside Saj in a small shop so over-loaded with goods that a sudden attack of claustrophobia made it hard to breathe. Each wall had shelves running up to the ceiling, and the door behind him was so slender as to be nearly lost. Everywhere he looked lay odd little things that were out of place. Here a small pile of Scrabble letter tiles; there a doll dressed in a pink satin dress, pristine and perfect down to her glass slippers and pink polished finger-nails but missing her head. Zane tapped at the plastic silvery tiara balanced on the neck, pushing it over.

"That wasn't so bad," Saj whispered to him. The older boy maneuvered through the piles of stuff towards a small, easily overlooked desk, piled with yet more junk. "Don't stare at her, okay?"

Zane opened his mouth to ask why, curious over who Saj might be jealous of, when Nifty walked in from some other hidden entrance behind the desk. His stomach rolled at the sight of her face. He quickly averted his eyes. There was no risk of staring; he never wanted to glimpse it again. The lower half of that face dripped down like melted wax, hanging loose and boneless for almost a foot.

"Saj, what have you brought me tonight?"

Her voice turned every word into a lyric that tugged at his insides. Zane had never heard anything more beautiful. It belonged to something else, and it troubled him to know that hideous Nifty was the one who possessed it.

"Pharmaceuticals." Saj glanced over his shoulder at Zane. "I think some of them are painkillers." He emptied the backpack onto the desk.

"Not the boy too?"

Zane shuddered and hoped she had meant that as a joke.

"Truly a nice haul. Do you wish to sell everything?"

The two boys' eyes met for a moment, Zane's wide and pleading, Saj's half-lowered above a grin. "No, not all the painkillers."

Zane whispered a low "Thanks."

"So what will it be? I have some cash today."

"What's in the box?" Saj asked.

One of Nifty's hands rested on a small metal tin. *"I'm not sure, actually. Another forager brought it in, and I could not resist a mystery."* She tapped the top with a pale fingernail.

"No key?"

"Combination lock. I'll probably have to have Caleb take care of it; whatever's inside will probably be a disappointment and not worth his fee, but..." She trailed off.

"Who's Caleb?" Zane asked casually, though he didn't really care what the answer was. Standing in front of Nifty and keeping his eyes everywhere but her was becoming burdensome. He wanted Saj to take him back to the apartment, share some pills, touch him again.

Saj spoke without looking back at Zane. "He's an Opener, and trouble. Basically can open up anything, and I mean anything." He pulled a folded scrap of paper from his pocket. Zane glanced over Saj's shoulder to see a short list written in penciled tiny letters. "I'll take a hundred in cash, small bills. Then some batteries. Lightbulbs. A couple tins of lighter fluid. Carton of cigarettes—"

"You smoke?" asked Zane. He had tried cigarettes in junior high a few times. They had left his mouth and throat burning as if he'd swallowed acid.

"No, but they're a great trade, so I always stock up." Saj glanced around the room distractedly before focusing again on Zane with a smile. "You need anything?"

Zane wanted to say "an understanding of Inside," but simply shook his head no.

ZANE LOOKED OVER HIS SHOULDER TO SEE SAJ LAGging behind. He began to slow down even though a growing sense of impatience filled him, one that threatened any moment to sour into maybe real anger. Hours ago they had argued in the apartment, coming close to shouting.

The routine he had fallen into with the older boy had worn thin. All Saj ever wanted to do after a day of scrounging was head back to that tiny hole of an apartment and lecture endlessly about whatever dangers they had seen or not seen or maybe might have seen. Then they would spend an hour or so wrapped in each other, with Zane never quite knowing what Saj wanted him to do. Some nights he simply rubbed the older boy's back and kissed him. Then Saj would fall asleep, leaving Zane awake for hours, wondering what was happening on the streets below.

That curiosity had festered within him over the last few days, until he felt trapped. Tonight he had needed out. Before he had run away to the Fallen, all he had ever heard was that it was a cool place. Sure, there was weird shit, but the stories were always amazing and left him wanting more. He had spent too long here avoiding every thrill except the one that Saj offered nightly. Tonight he had begged to go out, and when Saj started to shake his head no, Zane was ready to walk out. He almost did, and Saj must have realized it because he finally relented.

Along the way, Saj broke the silence between them by talking about clubbing in the Fallen. The raves had the intensity of fireworks, shining but short-lived and over before you were ever satisfied. Most were seedy excuses to drink and dance, to celebrate another day of survival.

Saj caught up to Zane. He tried briefly flashing his familiar grin, and Zane felt instantly guilty at how he had treated the other boy. He almost moved to throw his arms around Saj, hug him tightly and tell him that everything was okay, and suggest that they head back home and fall asleep in each other's arms. But that was fairy tale truth. Even if they did turn around, Zane would regret missing the rave that night, and things would only get worse. Why couldn't Saj understand that?

Zane idly tugged at the orange T-shirt he wore. Saj spoke up. "You look great."

"Stop. You always say that." Blushing slightly, he looked down at himself, at the clothes that Saj had spent days finding for him, ones with designer labels that were a thousand times nicer than the stuff he had worn on the outside.

When they reached a spot where they could hear the music, one ear catching the beat of techno, the other the notes of house, Zane looked up and saw his desire: down the block, a concrete dream bedecked with strings of white and red lights, three levels promising hours of delight, drink, and dance.

"Tomorrow," Saj said behind him, "it will once more be the remains of a parking garage, or maybe something's lair, or maybe disappear totally. But tonight, here's your club."

"Cool" was all he said as Saj took him in.

The club had no name—why bother with something so permanent when you had only a few transient hours of darkness to wring some pleasure from? The floor trembled from the beat of the music, emphasized by countless footfalls. With the dim lighting, everyone looked young and wild. Where had this crowd emerged from? Zane had never seen many people during his days spent in the Fallen Area, never more than maybe six or seven at any one time. But here was a horde, with swaying hands, bouncing heads, tiny signs of shared ecstasy. He couldn't help but gawk at them.

"I need a drink," muttered Saj, and walked toward the many amateur-looking bars, nothing more than a row of grownup versions of lemonade stands. Zane gazed once more at the crowd, tried to narrow his focus to a single body but failed. Feeling almost giddy, he followed after Saj.

They went to the nearest stand with its pitchers of radiator-green mix, ice bobbing up and down. The cardboard sign, marked with calligraphy in a green marker, read: Rad and bad for only $2 or Trade. A young boy worked the stand, his head shaved, the too-tan scalp marred by a black tattoo that Zane figured was some Chinese letter. He poured out the mix into two glasses, one a wine glass with a chipped stem, the other short and uglier than the rest. Saj reached for that one. Zane took the other, noting that there was another weird tattoo on the back of the boy's hand. He let Saj pay for the drinks with four dollar bills.

The mix tasted sickly sweet on the first sip, but the second went down milder and Zane felt an inaugural buzz. He drank the rest quickly, wanting to rush the feeling.

"Let's dance." He tugged at Saj's sleeve.

"I'm not a dancer."

"Please," whined Zane, but Saj shook his head and so Zane handed over his empty glass and eagerly slipped into the crowd, glancing back only once to see Saj walk over to distant wall.

Let him stand there and mope if he wants, Zane thought. Let him, and me, be alone for a while. He closed his eyes and moved to the many beats: the one coming from the speakers; the pulse rising from the stomping; and, distantly, the rush in his ear from his quickened heart.

When he had lost track of the music and his breathing became heavy, Zane broke apart from the mass. Walking away was almost painful; what might have been hours of dancing had created a link to the sweaty, writhing crowd. But he felt thirsty and sapped; he needed another drink, or maybe to have Saj help him find whatever passed for E around here.

He found the other boy still leaning against the wall, looking grim. He didn't even smile when Zane came near. Why couldn't he just enjoy himself? He looked almost pained, and held onto his right arm as if nursing a sprain. One of Zane's sneakers stepped on something that crackled and he saw by his feet the shattered remains of the wine glass. Next to that a splotch, a familiar red color with the remains of spindly legs sticking out at the edges.

Why the cutting now? Zane fought to keep calm, refusing to get overwrought and ruin his first night out in ages. "You okay?"

Saj nodded once, absently. "Yeah. Sure."

Zane inwardly groaned. Getting Saj involved seemed impossible. "Thirsty? I want to get another drink."

The other boy shook his head as he reached into a pocket for money.

He left Saj and went over to a different stand. A thin and kind of pretty girl stood behind it, with black hair that hung in damp ringlets. Her wrists were lovely, with lots of copper bracelets. She wore a tank top, white with a red crescent in the center, over cargo pants.

She smiled at him. Zane instinctively responded with a grin.

"So what's in this?"

"I made it myself." Her voice almost squeaked. "Take a sip and maybe then I'll tell you all the ingredients." She poured a little bit of murky syrup into a Styrofoam cup. He drank it like a shot, trying to impress her without really knowing why. It tasted a lot like flat cola. He wiped his mouth with his arm and held out the cup for more. "It's good," he lied.

She giggled. He noticed that her breasts danced for him when she laughed. "How do you want to pay?" She quickly took the sign from the pitcher and put it behind her back.

"Umm, what's the price?" He felt his face beginning to redden under her hungry eyes, but he didn't turn away.

"For a full glass?" She cocked her head to the left, as if in thought. "At least a kiss." The tip of a pink tongue darted out for a moment to moisten her lips.

"Pay her with the cash." Saj's words as he arrived were low but both Zane and the girl heard him.

Zane cringed at the coarse tone in the older boy's voice. "Maybe I'd rather kiss her."

"Rather than me?" Saj put his hand on Zane's arm. His firm grip reminded Zane how much stronger the other boy was.

The sudden and obvious jealousy shocked Zane. "What's your problem?"

"Do you think you're the first boy from Outside I've fallen for?"

Zane tried to shrug himself free, but Saj's grip tightened and kept him. "And I should care because?"

"You're the last. All the others... Well, they broke my heart." Saj swallowed to find more words. "So now, I'm asking you not to do the same."

Zane's face grew flushed; the words embarrassed him. All this because of some harmless flirting? And with some girl that he didn't even really care about. Or did that make it worse to Saj, a bitter hetero betrayal?

Out of the corner of his eye he saw the girl's wide-eyed expression. Her staring at them made his stomach churn. He growled at Saj, "What is wrong with you?"

Saj winced, and his grim expression changed. His mouth trembled. "Please...." He let go of Zane and used the hand to wipe at his eyes. "I—I think I love you."

Zane blinked rapidly, surprised. No one had ever told him that. To have this boy say it now almost scared him. "Love? Why are we talking about love?" He quickly reached out and grabbed the pitcher and lifted it to his mouth and took a big gulp. Then, with the stuff dripping from his lips and chin, he spat out, "I love this drink!" He nearly toppled it while setting it back down on the stand. "I love these tunes!" He turned back to the crowd behind them. "I love all of them!" He jabbed his hands in their direction. Finally he spun back to face Saj. "But don't tell me you love me. Don't you dare ask me to say it back."

Saj stared at him silently for a little while, then nodded once and walked away. Zane watched him leave, his eyes staying with the other boy until he was lost to the farthest reaches of the club. He felt suddenly sick to his stomach and wanted to sit down or, better yet, lie down someplace quiet.

"He looked upset." The drink girl stood next to him, holding a cup full of the stuff. She leaned up against Zane, bringing a hand up to twist around his arm. Her body smelled of perspiration and the flat cola drink. "Do I still get my kiss?"

He shook his head no, still looking off in the direction Saj had left. He just wanted to drift off himself for a while. But a hand pulled at his chin, turning his head so that her mouth could envelop his. At first he just stood there, passive, parting his mouth only so it could be over soon. Her tongue slipped over his teeth, cautiously sliding back and forth, skimming over his own. Then it all turned wrong. Hands gripped the back of his head, pressing their mouths together almost painfully. She moved around faster in his mouth, whipping at the insides of his cheeks, as if she had somehow added a few more tongues to push the kiss over the edge. He winced, tried to push her off him, but she held tight.

His nose struggled to draw in air to breathe, and he began to gag as a coppery taste swirled into his mouth and down his throat. He realized he had begun hitting her, his arms flailing, hands turned to tight fists as they fell again and again on her back and sides. But she ignored the protest, and after a few more moments still locked together, he felt himself weakening. Zane could swear his conscience whispered, "Stop fighting, stop resisting, let her have your mouth." He finally closed his eyes. The next thing he knew, he had fallen to the floor, landing on his side, feeling the impact on his shoulder and hip. He looked up and saw her smiling, looking pleased.

"Thanks, that was tasty." The tip of her pink tongue began to lick her bottom lip. Then another tongue slid out and moved over the top, leaving it glistening.

He gasped for breath and began crawling away from her. Someone rushing up to her booth stepped on his hand. He cried out weakly. She ignored him after that, going back to the stand, pouring out drinks, flirting with others. He reached the wall, managed to sit up. He threw his head back, purposely smacking his head against the wall. The pain felt welcome, wanted, deserved.

He felt like a total shit for treating Saj like that. No denying it. Why did the other boy even like him? His thoughts wouldn't settle down and his gut ached fiercely. When was the last time they had kissed? This morning? Last night? He suddenly needed to remember, but couldn't be sure. Zane strained to stand up, using the wall as support. He glared at the bitch serving her drinks, and then headed towards the door. He stumbled as he walked, suffering from all the elements that moments ago had seemed so amazing. The dim lighting made each step hesitant, unsure. The music disoriented him; it almost sounded like voices calling out, telling him to move this way, turn that way.

As he passed the crowd, they pulled at him, tugging and ripping his shirt, pinching and scratching at his arms and neck. He wanted to snap at all of them, but didn't have the strength. He could barely push open the door to the outside. He would go back to the apartment and apologize. Hell, he'd probably be on his knees, he felt so bad—that couldn't just be from what the girl had done to him.

He walked a bit, and then had to rest on the sidewalk, his head down between his legs to fight off lightheadedness. When he felt better, he looked around and realized he didn't recognize anything around him. Somehow he must have stumbled off in the wrong direction. He doubled back until he saw the parking garage and tried a route that looked somewhat familiar. He should have paid more attention to the way that they'd come.

Pale blue had crept into the edge of the dark sky by the time he found his way back to the apartment building. The edges of every sense felt dulled, his reaction time slowed until he might as well have been asleep.

He tried the door a moment before thinking that Saj would have locked it; when it opened, he stood there, unsure of what that could possibly mean. The apartment was dark. He trudged in, closing the door behind him as an afterthought.

He went to the bedroom, briefly considering stripping off his clothes and taking a shower, but every muscle screamed exhaustion. And he still had to deal with Saj.

A noise stopped him at the edge of the mattress. Something scurrying or rustling. He sank to his knees and moved onto the bed. Tiny legs scuttling over his arm sent him into a fit of shivers, and he cursed and shook off whatever crawled on him. His eyes were beginning to adjust to the darkness, and he could just make out Saj lying inches away, covered with a blanket.

Zane had closed his eyes to drift off when his entire right arm, the one stretched out closest to Saj, began to itch. The prickling soon became painful. He yelled and looked at his arm; things were crawling over his skin. He rolled off the mattress, slapping at his arm, knocking the things off.

When he stood up, the end of the chain to the overhead bulb brushed his face. He whacked at it wildly before realizing what it was. A tug on the chain and the room filled with yellow light.

What he saw made him scream. No blanket covered the other boy. Zane could barely make out Saj's shape underneath the strands of wet red silk. Spiders, countless spiders, with bloated bodies carried about on many legs, crawled over the wrappings and the mattress. Not far away lay a large knife, the sort you would cut a steak with, with strands of silk along the serrated edge.

Fuck! he thought. He staggered back, his back hitting the wall behind him. Saj's dead. Fuck, he's dead. He looked down at the knife, at the cheap wood handle, probably something the boy had scrounged up. Zane swept out an arm and knocked the crap atop the nearby dresser off onto the floor, but that wasn't enough, so he punched at the wall, cracking the cheap plaster and tearing the skin off his knuckles.

At the sound, the cocoon twitched. Zane stared at it. Now he could see no movement; he wondered if his guilty conscience had tricked his tearing eyes into seeing what he so desperately wanted. He had to know. He took a few steps closer, onto the mattress, carefully placing his feet to avoid the spiders. One of the awful things had perched itself atop where Zane imagined Saj's head lay. When he leaned forward, it brought up its front legs, waving the barbed tips in challenge. Beneath the spider, the cocoon slowly swelled, just an inch —maybe a breath, or a tremble.

"Saj, can you hear me?" he yelled. The spider moved an inch to the right, then back, sidestepping like a crab. The cocoon twitched again. Was that another breath? Had Saj heard him?

Zane slapped at a spider that came near. He went back for the knife. Down at the other end, towards Saj's feet, he began to cut. He pressed the blade lightly against the crimson silk, nervous about the risk of cutting into the boy underneath. A spider came near and he swiped the blade towards it, but it ran away along the length of Saj's wrapped body. Sweat dripped into his eyes, burning his sight, and he realized that the knife was sliding over the silk without biting through the strands. He pressed harder, and harder still, but nothing. He cursed and ran his own hand along the knife's edge, and cursed louder as it sliced the soft flesh of his palm. His own blood began to drip normally.

Frustration rose like bile in him, and he ran a hand through damp hair. He raised the knife to throw it across the room in angry despair, when an idea struck him. He brought the blade up and started slicing off thick handfuls of his hair. The cutting was easier than he expected. He took the locks into his hand and blew them over where Saj lay. They flew off on the puff of air, remaining whole and unchanged, landing on the silk wrappings like an orange garnish. He wordlessly cried out, tried again, but still nothing wondrous happened. There was nothing unusual about him, nothing special that could save Saj.

He needed help. Someone close by. He dashed out of the room, through the doors, to the elevator, stabbing the button. It would not come fast enough. He took the steps at a run, leaping down them three at a time. At the ground floor he headed for the broom closet.

Zane stood in front of Nifty's desk, keeping his eyes low. "Tell me how to find that Opener you talked about."

"*Why do you want him?*" She nearly sang the question, the last syllable raising in pitch with surprise.

At least she hadn't asked about the state of his hair. "Saj's in trouble. All my fault and I need help." He stared down at the floorboards.

"*Poor Saj.*" Real sympathy deepened her voice. He heard her rummage through the papers on the desk. After a moment or two Zane dared to lift his head a little. Her hands were writing a number on the back of an empty matchbook. He was momentarily distracted by the old gold wedding ring she wore. "*Here's Caleb's number.*" She held out the matchbook, but then swiftly pulled it back, out of reach. "*He's more mercenary than anyone, but he's also the best.*"

Zane didn't understand what she meant. When he reached for the matchbook again she let him have it. He eyed the number. Only five digits, with an asterisk between the 6 and the 8. "Is this right?"

But Nifty had gone, leaving behind only some wet spots on her papers.

He knew Saj didn't have a phone, and he didn't dare see if the rest of the apartments in the building were occupied, or if whatever occupied them would let him make a call. So he went out on the street, down to the corner, looking around in every direction.

An old man was walking with a much younger woman across the street. Zane went over to them to ask where there might be a nearby phone, but stopped at the last moment. He stumbled back a step when he saw her unsteady walk, each limb moving with stiff jerks. Both faces—one gnarled and leathery, in desperate need of a shave, the other utterly smooth and expressionless, with perfect cupid-bow lips —turned to look at Zane. The woman was a department store mannequin. The couple stared at him as he ran off.

He finally found a phone. It was in pristine condition, the metal shining as if just polished. There was even a dial tone. Still, he doubted the number would work. Nothing ever worked right, nothing was normal here. He started stabbing the buttons and realized tears were still running down his cheeks.

When he dialed the last digit there was no ring; the line went dead. He hung up and tried again, making sure to add the damn asterisk that he'd skipped dialing before. The line came alive and rang twice. He heard someone pick up, but they remained silent.

"Hello? Hello?"

The soft voice of a woman on the line answered, "I don't think I know your voice."

The Opener's name suddenly disappeared from his mind, and a moment of panic set in, making it hard to breathe or curse. Zane shut his eyes tightly to think. Caleb. That was it. "Is Caleb there? Please, I need to speak with him now."

"I'm his service. Do you want to hire him or is this a personal matter?"

Thoughts raced in Zane's head. What to say? While he did want to hire him, suppose he couldn't come right away. This was a fucking emergency and didn't you always give anything personal priority? "Personal. It's personal."

"All right. Your name, please. And give me your exact location."

He looked around. Nothing was familiar. He felt a sinking sensation in his stomach. He had gotten himself lost trying to find the phone. Why weren't there any damn street signs? "I don't know where I am."

A gentle sigh on the other end. "Calm down and describe something to me."

But the buildings all had that same telltale Fallen look: a slow but steady state of disrepair and decay. Menacing alleyways, choked with debris. The street empty—not even that weird old man and his freaky plastic date were still out there.

Then he caught sight of the boarded-up subway entrance. "Hold on." He let the phone slip from his hand, and ran towards the entrance. Graffiti covered most of the lettering—he was unnerved to see the word Moil spraypainted again and stayed well away from the stairs leading down—but he could make out a street name and number. He dashed back to the phone.

It took only seconds to pick up the receiver and bring it back to his ear and mouth, but the worry that the woman on the other end had hung up tore at his strained nerves.

"Good. I will let Caleb know." The sound of her voice calmed him. Then the line went dead. He didn't know if she had hung up or had been lost. He flashed the hook, heard some clicks, but nothing more.

He sank to the pavement, on his knees. He would wait. Just a little while. Then he'd call again. And again, until Caleb came to help.

"I don't know you." The voice from behind him startled Zane. "I'm not used to searching the Fallen for someone I've never met before." Annoyance could be heard in the words.

Zane almost didn't believe the young man standing there could be the hard-to-reach and troublesome Caleb. He was far too young, and looked almost sickly, with pale skin stark against the ebony turtleneck sweater and gray jeans. The thin face had never been touched with a razor blade; the feminine lips were a touch darker than the eyes.

"Say something."

Zane climbed to his feet. "I'm sorry, but I needed you now. It's an emergency—"

Caleb smirked. "Why is it always an emergency?"

"But my friend's dying. You have to help him." Zane aware that he was crying again. "Please."

"So how are you going to pay me?" Caleb reached out and threaded his fingers through the remains of the boy's hair. Zane shivered at the touch, at how it gently tugged at the surviving locks and then ran over the bare patches of scalp.

"Anything you want." Zane moved his head so that Caleb's touch became more of a stroking gesture.

The Opener laughed in surprised delight. "Really? Should you be offering something you'll regret later on? I'm not the sort that's satisfied with something once." Caleb's fingers slid down the side of Zane's face.

Zane swallowed his first words, unsure of what to say. He wanted, no he needed, to save Saj, but to do so would he have to abandon Saj for Caleb? He choked down a fresh sob. He missed Saj terribly, wished the older boy were there to hold him and tell him the right thing to do. But he was on his own for the moment, and the decision was never in doubt. He moved forward until they were inches apart and brought his fingers up to Caleb's mouth. Dark lipstick smeared on his fingertips. "Yes."

Caleb grinned around the boy's fingers. "Then tell me everything that happened."

Zane spoke quickly, rushed to say everything before his nerve failed. Caleb stood and listened, not saying a word, staring at Zane. When finally the boy began to repeat himself, worrying over whether they would reach Saj in time, the Opener spoke.

"Don't worry." He put his hand on Zane's shoulder and lightly pushed him forward, towards the closest building. "This will be quick." He took hold of the handle and opened the door...

...and they walked through into the bedroom. Zane looked behind him and saw the open apartment door. There were fewer spiders crawling about the mattress and over the wrapped Saj, but they looked twice as swollen as they had earlier.

Caleb kicked at the nearest spider headed for his black sneakers. "Shit." All the spiders' bodies split with an audible crack, leaving every one a twitching, oozing mess. Caleb leaned over to his right and threw up a little on the floorboards. "Ugh, that was nasty."

"Come on, get him out."

Caleb laid his hands, fingers spread wide, over the wrappings. He closed his eyes, as if to concentrate. A seam appeared at the head of the cocoon. It widened, and split the cocoon lengthwise.

Together they reached inside the cocoon, feeling the heat from Saj's body. His bare skin was slick with sweat and his frame looked gaunt, as if the spiders had drained him, turning his muscular form into something too thin. His chest rose and fell, though. His mouth was still clenched shut, his face rigid with pain.

Zane bent down and wiped clear the muck from Saj's face, working fast but tenderly. The older boy had still not opened his eyes or mouth, still looked half-dead. Zane worked his fingers around Saj's lips and jaw, prying open the mouth. Slender strands of the crimson silk had anchored themselves to the teeth and out crawled another spider. Zane bit his lip to keep from crying out, and reached down to grasp the spider in his hand. As he squeezed it, crushing it, he felt its sharp pinprick bites. Then it stopped, a wet mess in his hand.

Saj coughed then, and Zane put his mouth over the other boy's and emptied his entire breath into him. Saj opened his eyes, looking around blearily.

"Why the fuck did you do that?" Zane started crying again, but he didn't care.

Saj weakly lifted a hand, his fingers brushing one of the tears falling down the younger boy's face. He opened his mouth to speak but then ended up grinning instead, which quickly turned into a mix of cough and laughter.

"Touching." Zane couldn't tell if Caleb was speaking sarcastically or not. "Now let's get out of here." Caleb went to lift Saj up, but Zane pushed him aside and gently helped the older boy stand. He followed the Opener through the door again but they emerged on a different street.

"Down the block there's a shelter. Take him there." Caleb took hold of Zane's chin. "Don't worry, I'll be stopping by soon to collect my fee."

Before Zane could say anything, Saj groaned lightly. Zane adjusted the boy to bear more of his weight over his shoulder. When he glanced up, the Opener was gone.

"Tell me you won't do that again," he muttered, unsure whether Saj could even hear him.

In his ear, softly, he heard, "Tell me what I need and I won't."

Zane held onto Saj tightly as they walked to the end of the block. Zane's lips brushed the older boy's damp cheek as he answered "I love you." With every step, Zane repeated the words, feeling Saj's warmth spread through him.

CPSIA information can be obtained
at www.ICGtesting.com
Printed in the USA
FSOW01n1504180515
7135FS

31901056278742